GETTING THE GRINDER

AN ENEMIES TO LOVERS HOCKEY ROMANCE

LOVE ON THE LINE
BOOK THREE

BRENDA ROTHERT

Cover illustration by Elen Bushe

Cover design by Staci Hart

Edited by Rose Puls

CHAPTER ONE

Leo

"ALL I'M SAYING IS it would've been nice to know the only titties I'd see at this bachelor party are Isaac's," my teammate Lucien says as he cracks open a can of beer.

Isaac grins at us from the kitchen of the sprawling Breckenridge cabin we rented for Bash's last hurrah as a single dude. The main level of the cabin is wide open, the mountain view through the wall of windows in the main living area obstructed this afternoon by a blizzard.

"Wanna motorboat 'em?" Isaac, wearing only a pair of shorts, puckers his lips and circles his nipples with the pads of his index fingers.

"Pass," Lucien mutters.

Some of the guys have been sitting in the hot tub. When Carter walks into the living area, his hair is damp and a cigar is tucked behind one of his ears. "It's poker time, boys. I'll accept IOUs."

He cleaned all of us out last night, wisely drinking water while the rest of us got loaded. I'm nursing a hell of a hangover today and only drinking water. We have a rare eight-day break in December, and we're spending the first three nights of it on this getaway. After we fly back home the day after tomorrow, I'm pig sitting Carter's family pet, Darling, while he and his wife, Suki, take their girls to Fiji for the rest of the break.

"Let's do whatever Bash wants," Andrei, another of my teammates, says. "It's his bachelor party."

"It's not like there are many options," Carter says gruffly. "We're trapped here because of the storm."

Bash comes into the room, a beer in hand. "The plan was to stay here anyway. I don't want to go barhopping. I just want time with you guys."

I still can't believe Bash is getting married in June. With our schedules, this was the best time for a bachelor party. His fiancée, Lainey, is having a low-key get-together with her friends at their house. They're probably baking or something. She didn't want to get shit-faced in Vegas or anything like that.

"Are we gonna get snowed in?" our newest teammate, Anson, asks from the kitchen. "It's not letting up out there."

"Our rentals have four-wheel drive," Bash says. "We'll be fine."

"I'm not missing Fiji," Carter says. "I'll walk to the airport if I have to."

Anson comes into the living area and sits down on the big leather sectional, where I'm sitting with Lucien. He looks at me and grins.

"My sister hearted all the pics I sent of you. I'm sure they're all in her spank bank now."

I smile weakly because *fuck* is it awkward when he tells me his twin sister has a thing for me. He took pictures of me in the hot tub last night and said he was going to send them to her. Even though lots of people have seen me shirtless, both in person and online, it felt weird.

"Ugh." Isaac cringes. "I don't want to know who does it for my sister."

"Addison's been going on about Leo Abbott for years," Anson says. "She about had a coronary when I told her I was getting traded to Cleveland."

Carter catches my wide-eyed look of discomfort and tries to pivot the conversation.

"Who's in for poker?" he asks. "I've got more cigars and a bottle of Macallan."

"I'm fucking hungry," Andrei says. "Can we make something to eat first?"

"Hey Leo, have I told you what a great cook Addison is?"

Anson's question makes me tense up. He's my teammate and I don't want to offend him, but he's a hairy motherfucker with massive shoulders and a unibrow, and unfortunately, his sister looks exactly like him.

3

Not that it even matters. I'd never date a teammate's sister, because it would create problems.

"I'm not looking for anyone to cook for me," I say, shrugging. "No offense to anyone who wants to settle down, but I'm not there yet."

"Wait 'til you try Addison's meatballs. You'll break out a ring."

"I thought she wanted to try his meatballs," Bash quips.

I flash a murderous glare at him. He and Carter are my closest friends; they know how uncomfortable I am about Anson's attempts to set me up with his sister.

"Hey Leo, want to help me make tacos?" Carter asks.

"Yeah, sure."

Relief washes over me as I get up and head for the kitchen. Anson's sister has never even met me. I've tried to put Anson off from setting us up on a date every way I can think of, but nothing has worked.

"We've still got lots of toppings left from last night," I tell Carter as I scan the contents of the massive refrigerator, one of two in the twelve-bedroom cabin. "We can use the onions and peppers and olives."

Last night was our first night here, and we made homemade pizzas. Carter had groceries delivered to the cabin before we got here, and we had every possible pizza topping imaginable. Even grilled chicken, bacon and pineapple. The pineapple caused an argument over whether pineapple belongs on pizza. I'm not a fan of it, but I don't care if other people like it.

I couldn't believe how worked up Isaac got about it not belonging on pizza.

Bash's friend and future brother-in-law, Eric, is here with us, and he probably thinks we're a bunch of idiots after that showdown. He's sleeping now because he's not used to drinking like we did last night.

Carter and I are working in comfortable silence, him cooking ground beef and me heating up chicken, when Anson approaches, taking a picture of me.

"Addison's gonna flip when she finds out you can cook, too," he says.

"Enough, man," Carter says. "This is a bachelor party, not an episode of *The Bachelor*."

"Yeah, I know." Anson puts his phone in his pocket, smiling. "You guys need some help?"

"You can cut these up." I pass him several avocados, a cutting board and a knife.

I'm about to return to heating up the grilled chicken when I hear a scratch against the door that leads from an outdoor deck into the kitchen.

"It's that damned raccoon again," I say, picking up a towel and wiping my hands off. "I'm gonna wrestle that bastard if he got in the trash again."

Carter furrows his brow. "There's a fucking blizzard outside. He should be keeping warm somewhere."

I open the door, ready to take on a pissed-off trash panda, but when I look down, I find a shivering brown dog, her fur soaking wet.

"Oh, hey there." I squat down to pet her. "It's too cold out here for you."

Her dark eyes lock onto mine and my heart twists. Somehow I know it's a her, and she looks like she's walking a line between life and death. I think she's a golden retriever mix, and she's way too skinny.

"You're okay," I assure her. "Come on in."

She takes a few steps, glancing back outside. Then she sits down, still shivering.

Andrei brings a blanket and I wrap it around her. She won't move from her spot just inside the door, so I make a plate of cut-up chicken and bring it to her.

She scarfs the food, barely even chewing it. Anger rises in my chest as I wonder if this dog was someone's pet. Did they abandon her? She could easily have died out in this weather.

"Come on in." I try coaxing her with head and back pets, but she won't move.

When I bring her water, she drinks some, still looking out at the deck. We need to close the door to stop letting the icy wind in the house, so I slide my arms beneath her and pick her up.

She cries softly as I carry her over to the couch, where the guys have made a little blanket nest. Bash is starting a fire in the fireplace.

When I set her down and pull the wet blanket from her back, Bash says, "Oh, shit."

"What?"

He gestures at her belly, and my stomach sinks. Her skin is hanging loose and her nipples are enlarged.

"She's got puppies." I shake my head. "That's why she kept looking outside."

All the guys are gathered around now. Carter's our team captain, and he usually takes the lead on things, but I don't wait for him to say something.

"Everybody, get your coats and shoes on. We're going to find her pups."

Someone sighs heavily. "It's a fucking whiteout, man. We won't be able to see anything."

I look up, seeing my teammate Silas. He must've been in the hot tub, because his hair is wet and he has a towel wrapped around his waist.

"Stay here and sit in the hot tub, then." I glower at him. "I'm going."

———

EVERYONE COMES to find the puppies. The dog leads us to them, but it's slow going in the storm. It takes us almost thirty minutes to get to the tiny pups, who are curled up beneath a giant pine tree. There are seven, but only six are still alive.

Several of the guys pick up little fur bundles and put them inside their coats for warmth, and I carry the mama dog back to the cabin. We fill a bathtub with blankets and put all the dogs inside it.

Anson and Andrei go out in search of a warming lamp and dog food. I sit next to the bathtub and watch the puppies nursing. The mama dog sleeps, probably exhausted.

"I sent the girls a picture," Carter says from the

doorway. "It's been made very clear to me that I better not come home without one of those puppies."

"Darling will love that."

His pet pig, who was supposed to be a micro, is over four hundred pounds now. He's a happy, hungry guy who snorts loudly and rubs his nose against people's faces to show affection.

"So much for debauchery," I quip.

"Suki, Lainey, and Mara are taking a knitting class. So they're not getting too wild, either."

"Maybe Mara will accidentally stab herself to death with a knitting needle."

Suki's best friend hates me, and the feeling is mutual. Mara is an overly opinionated, high-strung shrew. I get along with pretty much everyone but her.

"Suki said Mara wants to knit herself a bikini top."

My mental image of Mara with a knitting needle buried in her chest is replaced by one of her in the shower, water trailing over her perfectly round tits. I only saw them for a split second when I accidentally walked in on her taking a shower and cemented her hatred of me, but it was long enough to know they're flawless.

Carter laughs, and I look up at him from my seat on the floor by the tub.

"What's funny?"

"Should I leave you alone with your thoughts about the woman you supposedly hate in a skimpy bikini top?"

I scowl at him. "I was imagining her bleeding to death."

"Sure you were."

I scowl at him. "I admit she's hot, but I'd rather fuck ... absolutely anyone else."

Carter considers. "George Washington?"

"Like alive and in his prime, or his corpse?"

He barks out a laugh. "You saying you'd rather cornhole him in his prime than Mara?"

No. "Maybe."

"You two have been at each other's throats long enough. Make a peace offering."

I scoff. "Yeah, right. I know she's smart about lots of things, but she's just not that deep, man. She's all about her looks and being snarky and materialistic. Classic mean girl. I don't want her to like me."

He shrugs. "Suit yourself. You need help with the dogs?"

"No, I'm good. Close the door when you go. I don't want Anson taking pictures of me."

Once I'm alone in the bathroom, I stand up to stretch my legs. There's a little cry from inside the tub and I check on the puppies. All of them are curled up around each other for warmth, most of them asleep.

I once did body shots of tequila off the navels of every woman on a college cheerleading squad. I was twenty-two, and it was a contest between me and a teammate to see who could do more shots. I won and then passed out on the bar floor. But I was up and at 'em again the next day.

I've never been the fastest player on the ice or the best shooter. But whatever team I'm on, I'm always the hardest worker. Up earlier than everyone else to get in an extra workout. Staying late at practice to keep running drills. It's how I keep my place on the team.

My motto when I was younger was "work hard, play harder." Now that I'm approaching thirty, though, I like my downtime. I read books and drink a lot less alcohol. And apparently, I hang out with puppies in bathrooms at bachelor parties while others are partying.

Works for me.

CHAPTER TWO

Mara

"I KNOW your workloads are heavy, but I can't get the board to even consider lifting the hiring freeze," my boss Gayle says. "We're going to have to stay selective about which cases we can move forward with."

I exchange a quick look with Jayden, the attorney I work alongside every day in the Cuyahoga County state's attorney's office. The two of us handle nearly all of the criminal cases in the lowly traffic division, but we're both too stubborn to do what our boss is suggesting.

The cases that take the most time and resources for us—things like driving under the influence and hit-and-run—are also the hardest to get convictions for. With our department down several attorneys and staffers, we could lighten our workloads by not charging as many of those cases.

But fuck that. I didn't take this job so I could bust the balls of people who were driving ten over the speed limit. I'm here to get drunk drivers off the streets.

"Mara, can you stay?" Gayle asks me when the meeting ends.

I sit up straighter, running a hand down my light-blue button-down shirt. It hasn't even been a year since I made the switch from working at a soul-sucking corporate law firm to this job, and even though I know I'm doing good work here, it's still nerve-racking to be singled out by my boss.

"How's it going?" Gayle asks me once we're alone.

I smile. "Good. Jayden and I make a great team. Missy is amazing, too."

The assistant Jayden and I share, Missy, has worked in this office for twenty-seven years, and she's the glue that holds us together. She knows all the things Jayden and I are still learning.

"I noticed you and Jayden are putting in a lot of hours."

She sounds less than thrilled about it, which is...unexpected. Our workload is intense, and the only way we can keep up is by staying late most nights and coming in on Saturday mornings.

"We have a good system." I deflect her question because I'm not apologizing for the extra hours.

Her dark eyes soften. "It takes time to dispo cases as

quickly as people who have been here for a long time. You and Jayden are both young attorneys, and I don't want you burning yourselves out. I wish I could shift more resources your way—"

"We're good," I assure her, lowering my brows. "I guess I should only speak for myself, so ... I'm good."

She nods, smiling softly. "I'm going to talk to Jayden, too. I want to tell you face to face that I'll be culling your filings for now. It's something I'm going to start doing for every division, not just yours. I don't want people in my office consistently working sixty-plus hours a week. It's one thing if there's a big trial, but you and Jayden have been doing it for months."

My stomach turns as I think about our office declining to charge on slam-dunk DUI cases. I start to protest, then clamp my mouth shut.

"Go ahead," Gayle says, looking amused. "I don't expect you to agree with me all the time."

"Can we decline more light traffic cases? I don't want to decline felonies to make room for misde-meanors."

"Of course. My only mandate is that you lighten the load so you can manage it in fifty hours a week or less. I want the two of you to decide what to drop, and you know I'll stand behind your decisions."

I breathe a little easier. "Okay."

"You'll also be working some domestics with Bruce."

My brows fly up in surprise. "Me?"

BRENDA ROTHERT

"You're ready. And Bruce is a great teacher."

Domestic violence cases can get messy. It's a department I hoped to work in one day, but it seems too soon. Domestics are a lot different from traffic. But with the hiring freeze the office has been under for more than two years now, flexibility is now a job requirement.

"I'll do my best," I promise.

"Of course you will. And you can always speak your mind to me, Mara. I know you're used to keeping your head down and getting along, but I want your opinions. Even if I can't unfuck this place most of the time, I still want to hear about the issues, okay?"

I nod, holding in a laugh. Gayle doesn't even know. I keep my head down and get along here because I want—need, actually—to keep my job. But in my personal life, I'm slightly...feistier.

"FUCK THAT GUY, and fuck his long dong silver, too," I say. "I'd bet my savings account it's more like *average* dong silver."

That evening, I'm at trivia with my friends Suki, Lainey, Dex and Harry. Our team, the Smartinis, is slaying the Men Behaving Badly category. In law school, one of my professors did an entire unit on Clarence Thomas's Supreme Court confirmation hearings. That's how his comments about his dick were unfortunately seared into my brain.

"You're willing to wager forty-one dollars on his peen?" Dex cracks.

I laugh. "And thirty-seven cents, baby. Fight me."

Suki orders us a round of waters as the trivia host starts reading the next question.

"This ironically named New York congressman got busted for lying about a photo of his—"

"Weiner," Dex whispers, cupping his hands around his mouth. "Anthony Weiner."

"Damn," I say. "You *beat* me to it."

"Was it on the tip of your tongue?" Lainey quips.

Suki grins. "The jokes are just falling out of the air on this one."

When the trivia round is complete and the host is doing rounds to check answers, we order some food. I get potato skins because there are literally no bad combinations of potatoes, cheese and bacon.

"How's the Bash-elor party going?" Harry asks Lainey. "Has anyone been arrested yet?"

"Oh, it's at the other end of the spectrum. They found a dog and her litter of puppies under a tree in the woods and they're taking care of them."

"No shit?" Dex asks.

"Apparently Carter's bringing one home," Suki says.

"A puppy?" I do a little clap of excitement. "Puppy bellies are one of my favorite things in the world. They're so warm and soft."

"Just like the head of a penis," Dex says, a dreamy note in his voice.

We all turn his way. My brows are lowered in question, and I'm sure everyone else's are, too.

"How did you...?" Suki struggles to even form a question. "You know what? Let's just move on."

"No one leave him alone with the puppy," Harry says.

"You guys are dicks." Dex rolls his eyes. "You know I'm right."

It's been months since I touched a penis. Wait...I do the math. It's actually coming up on a year. I've swiped right on two guys since starting my new job, but they were both just meh first dates and nothing more. With the hours I've been working, I don't have the time or energy for even a hookup.

A man approaches our table and taps Lainey on the shoulder.

"Excuse me, I don't mean to be forward, but you're so beautiful."

"Thanks." She smiles and shows him her left hand. "My fiancé thinks so, too."

His face falls with disappointment. "Lucky guy."

He turns to me, craning his neck to check my left hand. I scoff and say, "Absolutely not. Have a nice night."

He leaves, and I admire Lainey's look for a moment. She really is beautiful, and being with Bash has brought a glow and confidence that makes her even prettier. Her hair is naturally a stunning bright-red shade, and it's up in a cute messy bun tonight. Her dark-green, off-the-shoulder sweater is a perfect color on her, and her light-brown booties add a little sass to her fitted, well-worn jeans.

I'm still wearing my button-down work shirt and black pants with black ballet flats. I do a ridiculous amount of walking at the courthouse, filing paperwork and going to hearings in courtrooms on different floors. It's rare for me to wear heels these days.

I'm not even thirty, and it's been forever since I felt remotely sexy. I like my job a lot, but it's heavy at times. I file and prosecute criminal cases that can affect people's lives long term. Most of my energy goes to work. On my only day off, Sunday, I do laundry, buy groceries and spend time with my friends.

Not that I don't get in other times with my friends, too. I always leave work by six twenty on Tuesdays, so I make it to trivia night. My friends are the only people I'm truly myself around.

Our server sets down a plate with Dex's grilled chicken sandwich, no bun. The side salad he ordered is just iceberg lettuce, no dressing.

"Looks amazing," Suki says drily.

He sighs softly. "I have to lose the ten pounds I've gained."

I nod as the server slides my plate of potato skins in front of me. "Same. That's why I ordered vegetables."

Dex just shakes his head. He's fussy about his waist-line. I don't have a diet plan, but I usually only eat dinner, which keeps my clothes fitting the same.

Harry got a massive cheeseburger, which is his

favorite food. Suki got cheese fries and Lainey got plain fries. We eat in silence for a couple minutes.

"How's Aden?" I ask Harry.

He brightens at the mention of his boyfriend. "Great. He's still in Chicago for work during the week, but I'm meeting him there this weekend."

"That'll be fun. So you're going to Chicago and Suki's going to Fiji."

"That's right," Lainey says. "What about your new puppy, though? Do you need us to watch it?"

"Leo's doing it," Suki says. "He was already coming to stay with Darling, and I think he's bringing one of the dogs home, too."

Harry groans. "Darling and two puppies? At the same time?"

"I don't know, I guess we'll see if he brings one. Carter told me Leo's forcing the guys to take at least one apiece, so none of them have to go to animal control."

I scowl. "Leo's the one who belongs at animal control."

"I don't get why you hate him so much," Lainey says.

"Wait until he walks in on you showering and makes a shitty comment about your snatch and then get back to me," I say.

Dex pulls his brows down in a skeptical look. "I think the comment was made after you laid into him and called him a desperate pervert."

"Which he is. That's like describing him as a man. It's factual."

"Okay." Dex sets down his fork and straightens his back. "But what if it's also factual that your bush needed some tending?"

My lips part. "How dare you take his side? I'll do whatever I want with my bush."

"I'm just saying. I don't get within five feet of bush, so I'm no expert, but I'm not sucking an unmaintained dick."

I exchange a quick look with Suki. She silently warns me not to lose my temper, but the train has already left the station.

"I was taking a shower, Dex. It doesn't matter if my pubes were a foot long—he shouldn't have walked in on me. And then!" I point at him. "Then. He stood there and *looked*. I had to scream at him to get out."

Dex shrugs. "Maybe he was shocked."

"Oh, bullshit. You're being a perv apologist."

"Do we need some more drinks?" Suki asks. "Why don't I get us a round of Cosmopolitans?"

"Nothing but water passes these lips until I lose ten pounds," Dex says.

"Lies." I glare at him. "You're a cum-guzzling whore and we all know it."

A hearty laugh bubbles out of him. "You're goddamn right I am. But cum doesn't have calories."

"It has carbs, though," Lainey says.

Dex's head whips toward her. "What?"

She bursts out laughing. "I'm fucking with you."

The rest of us start laughing, too, and Dex winks at me. I blow him a kiss because I know I was being bitchy. But nothing sets me off like Leo Abbott. He's an arrogant, glib, overgrown frat boy.

If he ever gets a speeding ticket in Cuyahoga County, I'll pursue the death penalty.

Okay, not really. But at some point, I'll find a way to get even with him for walking in on me that day.

CHAPTER THREE

Leo

"THIS IS what I get for trusting you, isn't it?"

I'm talking to a pig, so it's not like I expect an answer, but I'm immediately suspicious when I don't find Darling in the living room with me, where I'm sweeping up the dirt from a houseplant he knocked over.

It's my second day alone with Darling, Carter's new family puppy, and my new dog. I brought the mama dog home with me and named her Birdie because I love golf. The girls named their new puppy Noodle.

Between taking the dogs out and cleaning up after them and a four-hundred-eleven-pound pig, I'm always busy. How does Suki ever leave the house?

"Darling, get in here," I call over my shoulder. "I

21

know you're lazy as fuck, but you're acting like a toddler who just slammed a Red Bull."

He likes being talked to, so when he doesn't come waddling into the room with his massive ass wagging with excitement, I put down the broom and dustpan to go look for him.

When I walk into the kitchen, the refrigerator door is wide open. Darling is on the other side of the kitchen island, only his curly tail visible. Groaning, I move closer to see what he's into now.

He looks up at me, a block of cheese in his mouth. I shake my head and glance at the refrigerator.

It's ransacked. The pitcher of green tea I brewed and put in the fridge to cool is knocked over. It's dripping off the shelves of the fridge, a pool of tea on the floor. Several containers of yogurt have tooth marks, some of them completely smashed. A trail of tiny white footprints stretches across the kitchen, ending where Noodle is licking a container of yogurt.

I pinch my brows together and glare at the pig, who gives zero fucks about the messes he made. "So you can open the fridge. That would've been good to know."

His attention is back on the cheese. It's a big hunk of cheddar, and it's too dense for him to get a bite off of it. He sets the cheese down and cocks his head at me.

I bark a laugh at him. "You want my help with it? Yeah, I'll get right on that, bro."

He lies down and rolls to his side, unbothered, and I throw away the ruined food, wipe down the fridge and mop the tea from the floor.

"Okay, let's finish the plant cleanup. Then maybe you can stop being a dick for five minutes. I'm always sneaking you food, so be cool."

Suki showed me how to put him in his enclosure, which has thick metal bars and is filled with soft blankets and pillows. They had it built in their sunroom for when the whole family has to be gone.

I tried to get him to go into the enclosure before I left for my workout this morning, but he acted like he couldn't hear me. Wouldn't even budge. And while I'm strong, I'm not risking my back by trying to carry four hundred pounds of ambivalent swine.

Birdie is my shadow. Wherever I go, she follows. If I'm in the bathroom, she's waiting outside the door. If I leave, she waits by the door I went out of. I took her to Carter and Suki's veterinarian, who said she's probably around four years old, but she's an old soul.

She trails behind as I carry Noodle to the living room. Darling follows, then walks up the ramp at the end of the sectional so he can watch me clean up while lying on the couch.

"They needed a vacation from you, didn't they?" I hold up a chunk of Suki's giant aloe plant, which is oozing aloe from the tooth marks all over it.

He rests his head between his front feet, huffing out a tired-sounding sigh.

"I can't keep up with you guys. We're gonna have to work something out, man."

When I finish cleaning up the dirt and torn-up shoots from the aloe plant, I flop down next to Darling and look over at the plant. It's mangled. Suki won't be happy.

Darling scoots closer to me, struggling to move his bulk. He puts his head in my lap and I scratch behind his ears.

"Just please don't get the shits from whatever you ate. We'll have movie night tonight, but I'm not watching *Babe*."

He huffs, and I could swear he knows what I'm saying. The girls watch the movie *Babe* with him all the time, and while I've never caught it from start to finish while over here, I've seen parts of it enough that I know it well.

I order steamed chicken and vegetables from a local Chinese place on my phone, and just as I'm hitting the button to pay for it, I smell something.

When I glance up, I see that Noodle just took a big shit on the floor. I look at Darling, who's smiling.

"Why did I agree to this?" I mutter. "I could have hired someone and enjoyed my break. I could be out on a date with Kelsey right now. She likes it in the ass, man. No strings. Just dinner and sex and see ya next time."

I get up to gather what I need to clean up the mess, stopping when I lock eyes with Mara. She's standing between me and the kitchen, arms crossed, scowling.

"This may come as a shock, but Kelsey's faking. She had high hopes that a pro athlete manwhore would know how the clit works, but sadly, that athlete is you."

I groan. "What the fuck are you doing here? Did your broom break down?"

She rolls her eyes. "You've used that one more than once, but who's surprised? You probably can't even spell IQ."

Dressed in a black cardigan and pants with a gray shirt that comes all the way up to her neck, she just needs a pointy hat and a wart on her nose to complete her snarky witch look.

I continue my walk into the kitchen, glaring at her as I pass. "Seriously, why are you here? I'm already watching a pig and two dogs, there's no room for a pissed-off cat."

"Suki asked me to check on some of her plants."

I groan, picking up a roll of paper towels from the counter. "Make it quick."

"What happened to that plant? And why are you letting the dogs shit on the floor?"

"Jesus fuck, can I have the number of just one dude who has fucked you, so I can ask him how he managed to stay hard with you nagging at him with that voice?" I make a dramatic face and imitate her voice. "Why are you thrusting like that? You're doing it wrong. I never gave you permission to enjoy this."

She looks stunned for just a second before scoffing and shaking her head. "You run your mouth a lot for someone who doesn't know shit."

I bend to scoop up the liquid puppy shit, which she probably enjoys watching me do. "Do you need directions to the plants?"

"Have you been taking the dogs out?"

I stand and turn to face her, my blood pumping with anger. "Do you want to do it? I can leave if you feel like you need to take over."

"I have to work. But I don't want Suki and Carter coming home to a destroyed house." She picks Noodle up and kisses his head.

No one bugs me like Mara does. She has a superiority complex and is about as nurturing as a cactus. I need to be the mature one and not fall into the traps she sets to annoy me.

"Look, I didn't plan on taking care of a pig, a dog and a puppy, and it's been a shit show at times. I can't get Darling to go into his crate and I'm taking both dogs out once an hour."

She wrinkles her nose and holds the puppy out in front of her. "He smells like shit."

A choking, gagging sound draws my attention to the couch. Darling's sitting there, a giant pool of puke in front of him on the couch.

"For fuck's sake, Darling." My shoulders sink. It's all I can do not to laugh at this point.

"What has he eaten?" The snark is gone from Mara's voice—now there's just concern.

"Sweet potatoes, cheese, yogurt, maybe some green tea ... and part of that plant."

I go into the kitchen and throw away Noodle's shit mess, wash my hands and dry them, and walk back into the living room. Mara's standing beside the plant, reading something on her phone.

26

"It's an aloe plant." She looks up at me.

"Yeah."

A little crease forms between her brows. "They can be toxic to pigs."

I exhale heavily, a knot of worry forming in my stomach. "Fuck."

Mara goes over to Darling and runs a hand over his back, looking at me. "The vet's phone number is on that list on the side of the fridge. Go call and ask what we should do."

I go into the kitchen and call the number, but it goes to voicemail because it's after hours. I leave a message and then call Caroline, our team doctor.

"How much of it did he eat?" she asks after I relay the situation.

"I don't know." I rub my unshaven jawline, feeling sick. "I have to fix this. He's a family member. The girls will never forgive me if he dies on my watch."

"With his size, I think he'll be okay. There's no direct treatment, but you need to monitor him. He'll probably have more vomiting and also diarrhea. If he gets lethargic, call me immediately. My biggest concern is dehydration. Don't give him any food. Check in with me in the morning and I'll come look him over. I can't give him fluids, but I can call in a vet to do it at the house if needed."

"Okay, thanks."

I go back to the living room and tell Mara what Caroline said. I'm expecting her to unleash her substantial fury on me, but she surprises me by staying calm.

"I don't think we should say anything to Carter and Suki," she says. "Suki's been looking forward to this trip, and they'll want to come home."

I exhale heavily, looking at Darling. "This is my fault. I can't even think about him not being okay."

"Let's not go there. Your doctor said she thinks he'll be okay."

"Yeah." I look at the pig, wishing he could tell me how he's feeling. "Pull through this and I'll feed you Goldfish while we watch *Babe* as many times as you want."

Mara clears her throat, giving me a look that says *You're a fucking weirdo*. "I think we should spread towels and blankets on the floor."

I meet her gaze, our verbal sparring forgotten. "You're staying to help?"

"Suki's my best friend. And I love Darling. Of course I am."

I'm relieved for the help, even if it is from the woman who drives me mad every time she opens her mouth.

"I'll buy them a new couch," I say. "Once this is over."

"Don't worry about the couch. Just focus on Darling."

Birdie comes up and sits down beside me, so close she's brushing against my calf.

"Hey, girl." I bend down to pet her. "You ready to eat?"

Darling gets all the way up and backs his way to the ramp, coming down to the floor. His legs are shaky and his smile is gone. I feel like such an asshole. Even though I didn't know the plant was toxic, and I *really* don't know why he never tried to eat it before, this is on me.

He walks one step before dropping a massive load of diarrhea on the floor, complete with squirting sounds. I sigh softly and walk into the kitchen without a word.

So much for movie night. There's nothing in store for me but shit, shit, and more shit. But as long as Darling's okay, I won't complain.

CHAPTER FOUR

Mara

I OPEN MY EYES, squinting against the light flooding the living room from the second story windows.

It was a long night. Leo and I finally both crashed on the sectional, Darling between us. The pig is snoring softly as I push myself into a sitting position, my neck protesting after the awkward position I slept in.

"Hey." Leo blinks at me, bleary-eyed.

His voice is raspy and his hair is messed up, his dark stubble completing his exhausted look.

Darling keeps snoring, ignoring us. Birdie, who was curled up on Leo's other side, gets down from the couch.

"Shit, where's Noodle?" Leo springs off the couch.

After snorting softly, Darling lifts his head from the

31

couch to see what's keeping him from sleeping. I pat him on the back.

"Come on, big guy. Let's go outside and stretch your legs."

There can't be anything left inside his stomach. The stench of shit hangs in the living room even though I took any soiled towels and blankets straight to the laundry room for washing.

We took turns for most of the night. One of us would do Darling duty while the other one did dog duty. Noodle cried nonstop when we tried to corral him with a puppy gate, so we had to either listen to it or let him out and keep track of him. And also, let him out to potty constantly.

"Noodle, you dick," Leo says from another room. "You're supposed to piss outside."

When I glance at my watch, I see it's six forty a.m. I have just enough time to let Darling out, move towels from the washer and dryer, and go home to shower and get ready for work.

Today is a long day of traffic hearings. I'm using my lunch hour to work with Bruce on domestic cases. I'm going to need a double at the coffee shop: a large coffee and an espresso.

"Darling." I add the note of sternness to my voice that Suki sometimes uses. "Let's go."

He huffs and slowly hefts himself up. I pee quickly while he makes his way to the door that leads out to the backyard. My coat is hanging over the back of a kitchen chair, where I left it when I got here yesterday, so I slide it on and walk outside with him.

It's freezing. My breath clouds in front of my mouth as Darling meanders around the yard.

He's walking fine and acting like himself, but I'm still worried about him. He lost a lot of fluids overnight. After a couple of minutes, he walks back up the deck ramp that leads him to me. He snuffles at the bottom of my black wool peacoat while I scratch his ears and enjoy a few more breaths of fresh air.

"You be good today," I tell him.

Leo comes out the door to the yard, brows lowered. He's holding Noodle out in front of him with both hands like the puppy is a bomb.

"You okay?" I ask.

He glowers at me. "This dipshit slipped in his own shit. I swear to God I'll pay whatever I have to for someone else to do this next time."

I don't let my amusement show, but I'm not *not* enjoying this. Leo's always cool and collected. It takes a lot to get him going, but this situation is sapping his sanity.

Which I get. It's a lot. I want nothing more than to take a shower, crawl into my own bed and sleep all day.

"Darling didn't potty, but he's acting fine."

Leo sets Noodle down on the frost-covered grass and turns to face me. "Good. I'll ask Caroline to come by and take a look at him."

"I have to go get ready for work." I close the sides of

my coat to ward off the cold, tucking my hands beneath my arms. "I'll be back after work, though."

Leo's only wearing dark-gray sweats, a T-shirt, a flannel, and tennis shoes, but he doesn't seem as cold as I am.

"You sure? You already helped a lot."

I nod, my nose turning into an ice cube. "It's not benevolence. I don't trust you alone with Darling."

"Right. Because I should've known the plant that's been sitting in the living room forever was toxic to pigs."

It's a fair point, but rather than concede it, I move on. "No one's coming over later or anything, right?"

He furrows his brow, puzzled. "Caroline will be. Why?"

"I meant like a hookup. I don't want to deal with any of that."

He bursts out laughing. "You think I'd invite a woman over here? Try to seduce her with the smell of shit?"

I shrug. "I don't know anything about your game, and I don't want to. If you'll be on your own, I'll help."

"Saint Mara to the rescue."

"Don't be such an asshole."

"Said the asshole."

Rolling my eyes, I open the door and let Darling inside. "My phone number is on Suki's emergency contact list. Call me if anything changes with Darling."

He flashes a smile. "If you wanted me to call you, you should've just said so."

34

I gape at him, then school my features into a neutral expression. "Not falling for it."

"Falling for what? We just spent the night together."

"Good one." I don't look at him as I walk into the house. "I'll see you later. See if Darling and Birdie can teach you how to spell *pig*."

"GFY, Mara. Go bust people over parking tickets."

I'm almost all the way in the house when I turn to glare at him. "Don't make fun of my job. You get paid to ice-skate."

"Good boy, Noodle!" He picks up the puppy and carries him into the house.

Once he closes the door, the smell of freshly brewed coffee makes me forget my anger. My nose latches onto the heavenly scent, drawing me into the kitchen like a cartoon character with heart eyes.

"You made coffee." I give Leo an imploring look.

"Yep."

"Any chance I could take a cup?"

"If it'll put you in a better mood, take the whole damn pot."

I go to Suki's mug cabinet and pull out her favorite travel mug, which has Ruth Bader Ginsberg's face on it. I'm so fucking tired, and not at all excited about an entire day of court hearings.

"You know I walked in on you by accident, right?" Leo asks as I fill the stainless cup.

Here we go again. We've litigated my humiliation in Carter and Suki's bathroom to death already, but he won't let it drop.

"By careless accident, yes. You were so drunk that you didn't pay attention to the sound of the shower running."

He's standing with his back to the kitchen counter, and he puts his hands on the counter on either side of himself. "The music was loud. I knocked."

It's still fresh in my mind, though if I could take an amnesia pill to forget it, I would. Carter and Suki had just had a new hot tub put in, and we all decided to get in it. Suki loaned me a swimsuit and I realized I needed to shave my legs and bikini area. Back then, I thought Leo was hot and I was excited about sitting next to him in a hot tub.

But then he walked in on me showering, and I freaked out. He just stood there, *looking* at me. I was horrified, so I screamed. I didn't want the guy I was crushing on to see me wearing a green clay face mask and shaving my bush. Which is reasonable.

I'm defensive by nature, and I went from embarrassed to pissed off in an instant. I should have locked the door, but he should have turned and left the millisecond he saw me. Instead, he gaped so long and hard I should have fucking charged him for it.

"It can't be undone," I say, securing the lid to the cup of coffee.

"So you're going to hate me forever?"

It's not that I hate him; it's more that I'm certain every time he sees me, he's picturing me in the shower with my foot on a bathroom shelf, a razor poised in front of my bush.

My legs were wide open. He got a better view of my vag than any man I've ever slept with. And it will never not be mortifying.

"I have to get to work," I say, avoiding his question. "Keep the animals alive until I get back, please."

He does an impression of a caveman, grunting and saying, "Me try."

I must be delirious with exhaustion, because I smile at his joke. But of course, I keep my head turned so he doesn't see it. Everyone else falls prey to his charms, but not me.

Not ever.

———

MY COLLEAGUE BRUCE'S tuna sandwich doesn't smell much better than Suki's house did when I left this morning. I grabbed a bag of vending machine Cheez-Its for our working lunch, but all I can smell in his small office is the half sandwich he's waving around as he talks.

"The caseload's generally pretty heavy," he says. "We plead out a lot of first-timers. The biggest mistake I see young attorneys make is not making deals."

His gray curly hair needs to be cut and there's a permanent crease between his brows. His dress shirts are often wrinkled and he looks frumpy, but Bruce is a cornerstone of the office. I've heard many cases of newbie defense attorneys who underestimated him getting schooled during hearings.

He brushes the breadcrumbs from his fingers, picks up a folder and tosses it to me. I'm sitting in a chair in front of his desk, and I pick up the file and look it over.

The defendant is named Paul Warren, and he's accused of stalking a woman. I'm sickened by the details of the case: he sent her as many as thirty-five threatening texts a day, was caught hiding in bushes outside her house, and tried to keep contacting her from jail.

"Thoughts?" Bruce asks me.

I glance up at him. "At the risk of being one of those young attorneys who won't make a deal, I don't see a reason to plead it. There's solid physical evidence and the victim is willing to testify."

He nods, almost smiling. "Bingo. Most cases hinge on the victim testifying."

He squints at his computer screen, something there catching his eye. "Hang on, I need to respond to this."

After putting on his glasses, he starts writing something. I take out my phone and check it for the first time since I got here this morning, finding a text and photo from Suki and a photo from an unknown number.

The one from Suki is of her and the girls standing on a sandy beach, ankle deep in pristine turquoise water. They're all smiling happily. Charlotte is wearing a T-shirt over her swimsuit, probably because she's a body-conscious preteen. A few months ago, she confided in me that some girls at school were calling her *Chunklet*, and I've never wanted to threaten and intimidate minors so much.

I text Suki a quick response, not mentioning anything about last night. She deserves to enjoy this trip. After last night, I have a newfound respect for how much work it is to take care of Darling and Noodle.

Birdie wasn't much trouble at all. She just doesn't like being alone, so she follows Leo everywhere. The other two, though, were a lot.

The other photo message is of Darling. He's lying on his back, his feet in the air and his head turned to the side. And of course, he's smiling.

There's a message with the picture: *Just to clear up any confusion, this is Darling, not the guy you hooked up with last week asking for Round 2.*

I suppress a sigh and put my phone away. Leo thinks he's hilarious. But if he's joking, that must mean Darling is doing okay.

Covering a yawn with my mouth, I stand up.

"I'm going to get a drink. Do you want anything?"

Bruce shakes his head. "I left some energy drinks in the lounge fridge if you want one. You might end up running laps around the courthouse, but you won't fall asleep, guaranteed."

"Perfect. Thanks."

I head for the lounge, hoping tonight is better than last night.

CHAPTER FIVE

Leo

"How was your day, dear?" I ask Mara when I hear her coming in through the kitchen.

Her answering glare is less withering than usual. I improvised a workout after she went to work earlier, the three animals watching me do push-ups, squats and lunges and licking my face anytime they saw an opening. Then we took a nap and I felt much more human after.

"Darling's doing fine," I say. "Caroline came over and checked on him. You don't have to stay if you need some sleep."

She sighs, her shoulders dropping. "No, I'll stay. I'm too tired to drive home."

Glancing around the room, she pinches her brows

together, looking confused. "It doesn't smell anymore. And the couch is clean."

I lift a shoulder in a shrug, bringing back my caveman impression. "Me not dumbass."

Her eyes glimmer with amusement. "I never said you're a dumbass."

"You just imply it by calling me a caveman and saying I can't spell three-letter words."

For once, she doesn't argue. She must really be tired.

"I need to get out of this house," I say. "I'll go pick up something for dinner."

"Okay, let me change clothes first."

She returns a few minutes later, dressed in leggings, a red T-shirt and slippers. Guess she and Suki are the same size.

"If I give you some money, will you pick up something for me?" she asks.

She's looking over her shoulder at me while pulling her hair back into a ponytail, the bottom of her T-shirt rising and giving me a better view of her phenomenal ass.

"Um, no." I force my gaze away and onto her face.

"Really? You're going to be that much of an asshole?"

"No. Sorry. What I meant was you don't need to give me any money. Just tell me what you want. You can pick the place since you kept our community safe from speeders all day."

Noodle is sniffing her feet, and she bends down to pick him up, snuggling him to her chest and kissing the top of his head. "At least someone around here is nice to me, Noods. Don't be mean to women like he is."

I smile. "Please. You're the queen of mean. Now what do you want for dinner?"

"A cheese quesadilla and two steak tacos from that Mexican place we all went to a few weeks ago. With a big side of guac. And also a brownie."

In addition to being hot, Mara's also a foodie. I've always secretly liked that about her. She doesn't order half salads when we go out to eat, like some women I know.

"Where do you want the brownie from?"

She shrugs. "It doesn't matter. I'd rather have one with walnuts and frosting, but I'll take what I can get."

I've spent a lot of time with Mara. I've seen her in fancy gowns, hockey jerseys and jeans, swimsuits, and even nothing that one time for a few seconds. But we're always with other people. I've never been around her without at least Carter and Suki there, and usually, Bash, Lainey, Dex, Harry, and the girls. Looking at her right now, in her casual after-work outfit, and talking about what we're having for dinner feels intimate somehow.

It's been a long time since I picked up dinner for a woman. I like my single life, and I have no plans to settle down anytime soon. But for a flicker of a moment, I wonder if Mara and I could have been something different if I hadn't walked in on her in the bathroom.

"The queen of mean is going to be a raging bitch if I don't eat soon," she snaps, breaking me out of my daze.

And *that* is why the two of us will never even be friends, let alone more. She's edgy and self-centered. What a waste of an amazing set of tits.

"Yes, Your Highness," I mutter.

I'm going to make the most of this break. Once I'm out of the house, I take my time walking out to my car. I don't have any kids, but I do have a baby—my white Range Rover SV. As a kid growing up in Elkhart, Indiana, I never imagined I'd own a new car, let alone one that cost two hundred grand.

My dad was an electrician and my mom worked at a jewelry store. With four kids, we always had what we needed, but no extras. I didn't have much of a social life in high school because I had to work so hard to keep my grades and hockey game at the level they needed to be for me to keep my scholarship to a private school.

It was a great feeling, paying off my parents' house for them when I got my first big pro hockey payday. I didn't ask them, I just did it. They would have refused if I had asked.

I squint as I approach the driver's side of my vehicle, seeing what looks like a scratch at the very bottom of my door. When I bend down to run my fingers over it, a jolt of pain in my left knee makes me cringe.

It's weird what does and doesn't trigger it. I'm pretty sure I know the cause, but it's going to have to heal on its own. I can't sit out with an injury. At age twenty-nine, keeping my first-line position gets harder every season. There are endless younger players willing to play as hard as they have to in order to take my spot.

And it wasn't even a scratch. The mark on my car rubbed away when I brushed my fingers over it. I get in and turn on some music, glancing over at the passenger seat.

Birdie always sits there, and she's left a little light-brown hair behind. When I brought her back from the bachelor party with me, I planned on finding her a good home. But I'm not sure how I can give her to a stranger, not knowing if they'll take good care of her.

I use my car's connection to my phone to call in an order to the restaurant, getting Mara what she wants and ordering ten steak tacos for myself. I'll eat the leftovers tomorrow.

After a stop at the grocery store for a few essentials, I find a bougie bakery and get a whole pan of brownies. When I walk into the kitchen with the food, her eyes widen over the dessert.

"Holy shit, with the flaky sea salt on top of the frosting? I may need to go change my underwear."

A corner of my mouth tilts up over her enthusiasm. "You get one now, and another one for every hour you don't make any shitty comments about me."

"Ha! Good one." She holds out her hands. "That would take at least a month unless you count the hours I'm asleep."

I unload the food from the Mexican place onto the

kitchen island, and she's eating her first bite of a brownie before I'm even done.

"That tastes better than sex feels," she practically moans.

I furrow my brow. "Who are you having sex with?"

"Only deaf men, remember? You once said they were the only ones who would be able to stay hard during sex with me."

I flick my gaze to hers, detecting a note of hurt in her voice. Which is weird, because she usually dishes out the insults much harder than I do.

"I shouldn't have said that."

She lifts a shoulder in a shrug. "I know I'm not for everyone."

"What's that like? When people don't like you? I've always wondered."

Rolling her eyes, she sets the brownie down on the counter. "Please. When I'm down, I look up Tweets about you and there's no shortage."

I shake my head and smile. "Did you see the one about me not being able to score in a brothel with two fists full of hundreds?"

"See it? I believe I retweeted it. And the one about trading you for a bag of used pucks is also a favorite."

I sigh softly as I unpack the groceries I bought. "Zero goals in the last sixteen games—Abbott is nothing if not consistent. Can't even score on an empty net. His shooting percentage would be lower than his GPA if he'd gone to college."

"Wait. Does that stuff actually bother you?"

I glance at her. "Did you want to grab a pen and paper and write some of these down for future use?"

"Fuck the haters."

I bark out a laugh. "You're one of my haters. So...fuck you?"

"*What*? You got a bottle of my favorite wine?"

She just noticed me pull the bottle of red wine from one of the bags I'm unpacking. I make a show of pulling a second bottle from the bag, too.

"Whoa! Are you calling me an alcoholic? Also, where's the corkscrew?"

I look around the kitchen, realizing something important is missing. "Shit, where's Darling?"

I sprint into the living room, where I find him lying on the couch, Noodle curled up against his belly. They're both asleep.

"I need to get a picture of that for Suki," Mara says from behind me.

Birdie pads into the room from the kitchen, sitting down so she's brushing up against the side of my shoe and ankle. She likes to always have some part of her body in contact with mine.

Mara takes a photo, then gives me a devilish grin. "We should prank Carter and Suki."

"I'm down, what do you have in mind?"

"Let's send them a pic of the two of us and tell them we've decided we like each other."

I bust out laughing. "They'll never buy it."

"Maybe not, but we should at least be able to get them to wonder."

"Carter will shit his swim trunks."

She turns and rushes into the kitchen. "The wine will help!"

I furrow my brow. "It'll help you, but what about me?"

When I walk back into the kitchen, Birdie on my heels, Mara is using a corkscrew to open the wine. I scoff.

"Thought you didn't know where it was."

"Foolish mortal. I always know. And I have an emergency corkscrew in the island just in case Suki moves this one on me."

"Bullshit."

Arching a brow, she sets it down, opens one of the drawers in the island, and pulls out another corkscrew.

I nod, impressed. "Your commitment to intoxication is impressive."

"God, you're annoying." She glares at me. "I'm not the lush you make me out to be."

"Sometimes you are. But I'm not judging. I've made an asshole out of myself while drunk before, too. Like one time I walked into a bathroom while a pretty woman was showering and now she hates me."

A smile dances on her lips as she says, "Get over here and make it look like you like me."

She holds up her phone, opening the camera and angling it for a selfie.

"We should kiss," I say. "That would convince them."

She clears her throat. "Just put your arm around me. I'll lean in."

I'm a lot bigger than her, so when she leans in toward my chest, my arm wraps all the way around to her stomach. I hold her close, not missing her intake of breath.

She's soft and warm, and I think she hates me less than she did yesterday. Her closeness makes me aware of my pounding heart. I've always found her very attractive, but I really do find her sharpness to be a turnoff.

Tell that to my dick, though. It goes from stiff to fully hard as she moves her long, dark hair in front of one of her shoulders, exposing her neck to me.

Her scent is light and citrusy, and I can't help drawing her in a little closer so I can smell it better.

"Ready?" There's a smile in her voice.

I smile and she leans her face against mine, her hair soft against my jawline. I have to remind myself that it's Mara, the queen of mean.

"Got it."

She steps away from me, turning her phone screen to show me the photo.

"Damn." I arch my brows. "That's convincing."

She pours herself a glass of wine and grabs a taco, taking both with her when she takes Darling and the dogs out to the backyard.

I stand at the island and eat several tacos, spending the entire time thinking about how addicted I could get to a softer version of Mara. When her claws are retracted, she's breathtaking.

But most of the time, she's prickly and downright hostile to me. This has to be a fluke I caused with the steak tacos, wine, and brownies.

Tomorrow she'll be back to hating me.

CHAPTER SIX

Mara

"Did you guys hook up?" Suki's expression is half-shocked, half-thrilled.

"God, no. I told you it was a prank."

She practically flew into the house after Carter pulled their giant SUV into the garage. The two of us are alone in a main-floor half bathroom, her carry-on bag still clutched in one hand.

"I don't understand. Why were you even here?"

"Well, it's kind of a long story, but you asked me to check on your plants."

She nods. "Yeah, but that probably took like five minutes."

"My Darling!" Young Hallie's exuberant greeting for her pet makes me smile.

"Come here, Noods. Aw, you're a good boy." That's Charlotte, the middle girl.

"The trip was good?" I ask Suki.

She lowers her brow in a look of confusion. "It was great, but I want to know how you ended up cozied up to Leo and not only were neither of you bleeding from a knife wound, you were both smiling."

That interaction a couple nights ago was pretty much the end of the camaraderie between me and Leo. I was so exhausted after dinner that I crashed in the guest room until I had to get up for work the next morning.

Leo slept in the living room with the animals, and I wasn't much help that night. Darling wasn't sick anymore, though, so it was easier than the night before.

I didn't need to come back over once things were smoother, but Leo texted me earlier today and asked if I could take over for him for the final two hours before Carter and Suki got back. That's why I'm here now.

"Darling is fine." Once she finds out their pet pig was sick, Suki's going to freak out, so I open with the good news. "But he did eat part of your aloe plant and it made him sick."

"What?" Her brow crinkles with worry.

"He's fine. Leo asked the team doctor to come look at him. But there was one long night of diarrhea and vomiting, plus a puppy and a new dog to take care of, so I stayed to help."

She balks at that. "You stayed here? All night? With Leo?"

"It was a literal shit show. We were constantly cleaning up shit and puke and trying to keep Noodle from eating the furniture."

Her expression turns shrewd and assessing. "But you still had time to pose with him like a happy couple for a selfie?"

"Well, that was the next night."

"I knew it." She crosses her arms, her smile victorious. "All this time I've been telling you that you don't hate him at all. And you deny it like Shaggy denies banging on the bathroom floor."

My jaw drops and my eyes bulge. "What the fuck? I come over to help with your pets and you compare me to a has-been reggae singer?"

"You slept with him."

I let out a short snort of derision. "I absolutely did not and would *never*. It was a joke. You know me better than anyone. Look at my face right now."

She locks her eyes onto mine and stares for a few seconds, silent. "Okay, so no sex, but your feelings about him *have* changed."

I shake my head adamantly. "Not really. He brought me tacos and wine, so maybe I hate him at like a nine point five instead of a ten."

She folds her hands and puts them beneath her chin, grinning. "You like him."

I roll my eyes. "I tolerated him because I was worried about Darling."

"Suki?" Carter calls out from the living room.

"I'm in the bathroom with Mara."

There's a pause before he says. "I don't even want to know."

I reach for the doorknob, but she bats my hand away. "You weren't just smiling with your mouth in that picture. Everything was smiling. Your eyes—your whole face, really. Even your boobs looked perkier than usual."

"What?" I gape at her. "Look, I know you love Leo and all, but he and I are never, ever getting together. Like ever."

"So you're saying I should wait to try to get pregnant so we can have babies at the same time. Maybe yours will have Leo's green eyes."

This time, my laughter is genuinely amused. "You're trying to bait me, and I'm not falling for it. I have to get back to work."

When I walk out of the bathroom, Hallie is snuggling with Darling on the couch.

"Where's Uncle Leo?" she asks. "I wanted to see Birdie."

"They had to leave early, but I'm sure they'll be over soon." I walk over to her. "How was Fiji?"

"Fun! We stayed in a hut with water underneath it. I went swimming every day."

"Every day?"

She grins, the gap from a missing tooth making me want to smoosh her in a hug. "And I ate pineapple cake and went to a waterfall."

"Sounds like a blast. Did you miss Darling?"

"Yeah." She climbs on top of him and wraps her arms around him. "Was he sad?"

"Nah. He did great, but I know he's happy you're home."

Carter walks into the room. "Hey, where's Leo?"

"He had an appointment to get to, I don't know what it was. And I have to get back to work, so ... Noodle went out to potty about fifteen minutes ago. The plants are all watered. Except for the aloe, which is in the laundry room—so Darling can't get to it."

"Hey, thanks for your help," Suki says.

"No problem."

I walk into the kitchen and grab my bag. Suki follows me and gives me a quick hug.

"My boss won't let me work late anymore, so I'm reading files at home," I tell her. "I'm buried, so I don't know if I'll see you until the next trivia night."

"Okay. Is this just a busy time at work? Is it going to get better?"

"It probably won't get better, but it's okay. I'm good."

She gives me a pointed look. "You always say that, even when you're not. And then the stress just builds and builds until you explode."

"That's how I'm made." I wave at her on my way out the door. "Tell Olivia and Charlotte I said hi."

"I will. Call me later if you want to talk about Leo some more."

I call out to her over my shoulder. "I don't!"

CHAPTER SEVEN

Leo

"HOW ARE YOU FEELING?"

I sigh heavily, trying to figure out how to answer. It's not something I can put into one or two words or even a single sentence. But that's why I'm here. I spend my entire hour-long sessions with my psychiatrist, Dr. Laudner, talking about how I feel, and I still never fully understand it myself.

"About the same as last week," I say. "I spent the past few days taking care of my buddy's pets while he went on vacation with his family. And I still have the dog I told you about last time. I don't think I'm going to be able to rehome her."

Dr. Laudner pushes his glasses up on his nose, looking pleased. "You've said you have trouble forming close attachments, but a pet can be just as important as a person in your life."

"Yeah. Birdie's great, but I didn't love being trapped in the house for four days. There was no escaping my own head. I couldn't get in good workouts. A friend of my friends came by to help, and even though I don't like her, it was just good to see another face."

"Are you feeling any differences with your new medication dosage?"

I shift on the loveseat I'm sitting on, shaking my head. "I feel the same."

"Still having intrusive thoughts?"

I look away. I fucking hate this. I don't like talking about my feelings, but these sessions are required for me to get refills on my medications, and I can't function without them.

For years, I refused to get professional help. I'd still be refusing, but I had a panic attack before a game last year, and our team doctor, Caroline, treated me for it. I thought it was a heart attack. I had to miss the game to go get tests at a hospital, and when everything else was ruled out, the doctors said it was a panic attack, and that those don't happen for no reason.

Yeah, no shit. I knew I was struggling, but I thought I was managing. Well, other than not sleeping well and having panic attacks.

Now that I'm on meds for my depression and anxiety, it's more manageable. I'm not fighting myself as hard as I used to. I don't worry constantly about getting cut from the team. But I still have issues, and now I have the additional worry that people will find out I'm wearing a mask and taking medications to keep me from falling over the edge.

"I've been thinking I'm not good enough my entire life," I say. "There's no medication that's going to change that."

The doctor nods. "What do you think you're not good enough for?"

I cross my arms in front of me, agitated. "You already know. My place on the team, my friends ..." I run a hand through my hair. "My whole life, I guess. It feels like I'm a fucking fraud and everyone around me is going to realize it. If I get cut from the team, I'll lose my friends. My parents will be ashamed of me. Even if they don't admit it."

Dr. Laudner is in his mid-fifties. He embraces his baldness, shaving his head almost to the skin. He does triathlons and makes homemade pasta. I like him. But I still don't like these conversations.

"Do you think your friends only value you because of your career success?"

I shake my head. "I know, I really do. I know they wouldn't tell me to fuck off if I got traded. But I'd live somewhere else. I'd be on a different team. It wouldn't be the same."

"You find change hard."

I shrug. "Yeah."

"What are some of the changes you've experienced in life that have been hard for you?"

I study the pen on his coffee table, considering stab-

59

bing myself in the eye with it so I don't have to talk about this. We've been over it many times. It's best to just get it out of the way, I guess.

"You already know the biggest one. Kyle."

"The death of a sibling is incredibly difficult, especially for a child."

I rub my chest and take a deep breath. Just thinking about Kyle is enough to bring on an anxiety attack, even on my meds.

"I just want to be normal. I mean, look at me. I'm six-three, I'm fit, and I'm a professional athlete. People look at me and think I've got my shit together. But I can't fucking stay in a room when a song by Foo Fighters comes on. I get physically ill."

"Why do you think that is?"

I take a few more deep breaths, the tightness in my chest worsening. "That was his favorite band. We listened to their albums all the time."

"Do you have happy memories of him?"

I scrub a hand over my face. "Yeah, of course. I need a subject change."

He straightens the frame of his glasses on the bridge of his nose. "Tell me about your new dog. Birdie, right?"

"Yeah. She likes to be with me all the time. I think she's afraid I'm not going to come back when I leave."

"Is she playful?"

"Sometimes. I'm trying to teach her to fetch tennis balls, but she doesn't like bringing them back to me."

He smiles. "I had a dog like that once. She'd fetch the ball and just keep running."

"I guess as long as the dog's having fun, that's what matters."

"That's a good way to look at it."

Before he can ask me another question, I ask him one. "Am I going to be like this forever? Are the medications doing as much for me as they'll ever be able to?"

"We can always try new medications and dosages. Tell me what you mean by *like this*."

"A mess on the inside who's trying to make it look like I'm fine to anyone who sees me."

He writes something down on his pad of paper. "What do you think would happen if you shared what's on the inside with someone?"

I hum a note of amusement. "They'd tell people. Think I'm nuts. Worry about me. Feel sorry for me."

"Is there anyone you trust enough to tell? One of your parents, maybe?"

I shake my head. "No, I'd never put this on them. They think I'm doing great."

"A friend?"

"If I had to pick someone, I'd tell Carter. But he'd see me differently, and I don't want that."

"You know, many people have anxiety or depression. Or both. A lot of the time, sharing it with someone you trust can strengthen the relationship."

I look at the clock on his bookshelf, eager to stop talking about something I'll never do. "Is it okay if I cut out a little early today? I have a team meeting later and I haven't been home from the pet sitting thing yet. I want to take a shower."

"Of course." He sets his notebook on the table next to his chair. "Do you want to stick with the new dosage and give it more time? We can try a different medication if you want to."

I stand up. "I'll stay with what I have. See you next time, Doc."

———

A LITTLE OVER AN HOUR LATER, I walk into the Italian restaurant where our team dinner is being held, seeing the long table filled with my teammates from the hostess stand.

"Hey, man." Carter smiles as he stands up to give me a one-armed hug. "I heard Darling gave you some trouble."

"Nah, it's all good." I take the open chair next to him and scan the table. "Is there bread coming? I'm starving."

"Yeah, I ordered bread and a bunch of apps."

"You managed to get a tan in four days?" I ask.

"The girls wanted to be in the water all day, every day."

"It was a good trip, though?"

He nods. "Yeah, it was great. Didn't realize how much I needed it until we were there."

Bash is sitting across from me, talking to Andrei.

The chair next to me is open, and I force myself not to react when Anson takes it.

"Hey, man. How's the new dog?"

"I named her Birdie. She's good."

He gives me a knowing look. "You were never gonna be able to find her a good home. I could tell by the way she wanted to be next to you all the time."

"Yeah, she's a sweet dog."

I inhale the scent of garlic bread and glance over my shoulder, hoping there's some arriving at our table soon.

"Do you have plans for New Year's Eve?" Anson asks.

"Uh ... I'll probably be doing something with Carter and Bash."

He grins, looking excited. "Addison's coming to town. Can we all do something together?"

Fuck. I just gape at him, unsure how to handle it. Then I clear my throat and recover.

"Hey, cool. I'd definitely like to meet her. But I am seeing someone, just so you know."

His smile drops away. "What? Bullshit. You weren't seeing anyone a week ago."

"It's brand new."

"What, like one date? That's not a serious relationship. Do you just not want to date my sister?"

I'm knee deep in shit. Anything involving me and Anson's sister is a minefield I'm not walking. Good thing I have a perfect excuse.

"It's not like that. Mara and I have known each

other for a long time. She stayed over at Carter's with me while he was gone, and we decided to make things official. We've been sneaking around for a while now."

Bash's chin is practically on the table. "No fucking way, man. Mara?"

It would be fantastic if he would shut the fuck up, but that's unlikely. I shoot him a look.

He doesn't pick up on it. "How did I miss that? You guys are so convincing with the hating each other act."

"We did hate each other until ... we didn't."

"I have proof." Carter turns his phone screen around, showing the guys the selfie Mara took of us.

Bash bursts out laughing. "What? How did you get her to stop hating you?"

"Well, Bash, when a guy has a big wrench and he knows how to use it, he can be very convincing."

"You're telling me you guys have ..." He looks over both shoulders and lowers his voice. "Fucked?"

I grin, enjoying his disbelief. "Many times. Many ways."

Bash looks at Carter. "Why didn't you mention this?"

"I just found out on my trip."

Bash takes out his phone. "Does Lainey know?"

Shit. If he texts Lainey, she'll text Mara, and Mara could come storming into this restaurant and blow my story.

"Mara wants to be the one to tell her," Carter says, saving me. "I saw her earlier today and we talked about it."

I shoot him a grateful look.

Anton looks almost sick over the news. "Addison's gonna be crushed. She wanted to kiss you at midnight on New Year's Eve."

"We can still be friends," I offer.

He nods weakly. "Yeah. I'll let her know."

I breathe a little easier, swiping a roll from the breadbasket as soon as it hits the table.

I'm saved. All I have to do is pretend I'm with Mara, and Anson won't try to set me up with his Bert-look-alike sister.

Well, I have to get Mara to go along with it, too. I wonder if I can convince her the tacos, wine and brownies were worth a favor of this magnitude.

I should probably have an entire case of wine in hand when I ask. And more brownies.

CHAPTER EIGHT

Mara

"Are you sure there aren't any new filings stacked up under one of our desks?" I lower my brows and look around the office I share with Jayden.

He gives me a wry look. "It's not the 1980s, so if there were more cases, this handy invention called a computer would let us know. I think we're—"

"No, don't say it! You'll jinx us."

"It's because we had Robson this week instead of Hampton. Robson don't play. She likes her courtroom efficient and on time."

"Hampton wasn't made for traffic court." I run a hand over the empty spot on my beat-up old wood desk where pending case files are normally stacked.

Jayden snorts with amused agreement. "He wasn't

even made to be a judge. Performance theater is his game."

Every time one of us says, or even asks, if our workload is *caught up*, it's like a Bat-Signal to drivers in the county to speed, run red lights and drive while blindfolded. So we try to be cool about it and not tempt fate.

It's 4:55 p.m., and we're going to be able to leave for the day. I could take some work with me, but after a long day of hustling hard in court, I'm not feeling it. Maybe I'll actually have an evening to relax.

"I think I'm leaving now." There's a questioning note at the end of my sentence because lately, Jayden and I take turns forcing the other to power down the computer by 5:15 so we can badge out before 5:30 and not get busted working late.

"I'm right behind you."

"You have plans tonight?"

"Dinner with Jana's parents."

I stand and grab my coat from the coat tree in the corner of our office. "Nice. You like them, right?"

"For the most part. Her dad has asked me at least fifteen times over family dinners why I bothered to go to law school to work at a job that pays less than seventy grand."

I scoff. "He sounds delightful."

Jayden grabs his suit coat from the back of his work chair. "Perks of our salaries being a matter of public record, I guess."

"No, he's being a dick."

"We've beaten the subject to death, so hopefully it's

over. My fantasy football team kicked his team's ass this year, so I try to steer the conversation toward that topic."

I walk out of our office and he turns the light off, locking the door behind us. We used to have our own offices, but we work more efficiently sharing one.

"How about you?" Jayden asks on the walk to the elevator. "Got any plans?"

"I'm going to enjoy the quiet of my apartment. Maybe catch up on some *Housewives*."

He cringes. "Jana loves that garbage, too."

"Well, not all of us are highbrow enough to spend our downtime rooting for pretend football teams."

"Okay, fair."

The elevator doors slide open and we step inside, several other courthouse employees joining us. Once we're on the first floor, Jayden waves and we head in separate directions. His fiancée, Jana, is a first-grade teacher, but I've only met her a couple of times. Jayden and I are friendly, but not friends, which is how I like it.

My coworkers have never seen me drunk and unfiltered, and I plan to keep it that way.

Light snow is falling when I walk outside. I button up my wool coat and pull my gloves out of my coat pockets, putting them on.

The crunch beneath my feet takes me back to a trip I took with my parents to Chicago when I was a kid. It was before our lives were upended, and I assumed all our days would be as magical as that one.

My mom loved the holiday window displays downtown, having visited them with her parents when she was growing up. We lived in Arizona, and I'd never seen snow other than in pictures.

I don't think I stopped smiling once that day. The crunch of snow beneath my shoes as we walked, the magical holiday decorations and getting to ice-skate outdoors with my parents as holiday songs played created a core memory.

They took me into a toy store and let me pick out a new stuffed animal. I chose a white unicorn with a rainbow horn. If I saw it today, I'd probably break down in tears. Memories of the good times are bittersweet.

My old, rusted Chevy sedan is parked a block away today, and by the time I'm almost there, my nose is ice cold. I squint at my car when I see that the windshield has already been cleared of snow.

Must have been a random act of kindness. I reach my car, take out my car keys and am about to open my door when someone steps out of the Range Rover parked next to my car.

"Hey."

The man's deep-voiced greeting makes me look over. I'm surprised to see Leo standing there, dressed in jeans and a brown Carhartt coat.

"What's wrong?" I ask.

A smile plays on his lips. "Nothing. Everything's fine."

I wait for him to explain. He shifts, discomfort flashing over his expression.

"Are you hungry?" he asks. "I need to talk to you about something. Maybe we could talk over dinner."

I lower my brows, suspicious. "Did something happen to Suki? Or one of the girls? I don't want to wait; you need to tell me now."

"No, they're fine. This isn't about them."

My heart races as I consider the options. None of them is good.

"Is it about Carter?"

Agitation flashes in his eyes. "No. It's nothing bad. I need to ask you a favor."

"Leo, if you agreed to pet sit again, I'm going to kick you directly in the balls. There's no way I'm helping you."

He shakes his head. "Will you stop? Just get in my car and let's go get some dinner. Anywhere you want."

I look him up and down. The jeans and coat are working well on his tall, muscular frame. The lack of a hat or gloves sends the message that he's too manly to be bothered by the cold. And the breath clouding in front of his face is making me imagine what his breath would feel like on my bare skin.

But it's Leo. He drives me crazy, and one night of great sex isn't worth him never letting me live it down.

It's *not*. I have to forcefully remind my sex-deprived self that riding him is a bad idea I'll regret later.

I unlock my car door. "Let me guess—there's a party in your pants and I'm invited? No thanks. I wasn't coming onto you with the prank. It was just a prank and it's over."

"Mara."

His stern tone makes me turn and face him. His expression is almost troubled ... like he genuinely needs something and doesn't want to have to ask me for help.

"Okay."

I lock my car and get in the passenger side of his instead. It has that heavenly, leathery new car smell and is pristinely clean. My car smells like coffee and is covered with cracker crumbs.

"Where do you want to eat?" he asks.

He looks so damned troubled that I can't help feeling bad for him.

"You don't have to take me out to dinner. Just tell me what you need. I can't fix anyone's court cases, though, if that's what it is. Not even a parking ticket. I could lose my job."

"It's not that." He wraps one of his big hands around the steering wheel and looks over at me. "You like seafood?"

"Yeah, but seriously, we don't have to go to dinner."

My car seat is deliciously warm, the heat seeping into my back and legs. I could have had a car like this someday if I'd been smart and stayed in corporate law. I'll probably be driving my beater well into my fifties.

"Well, I haven't eaten yet," he says, his eyes locked onto mine. "Have you?"

He really does have nice eyes.

"No."

He nods and puts the car in reverse, checking his backup camera. My heart is still racing over this unexpected development in my day.

"Are you sick? Do you need help breaking the news to Carter and Suki?"

He exhales through his nose, his lips turning up slightly in a smile. "No, it's nothing like that."

"Is someone suing you? Because I'm not the right kind of attorney for a sexual harassment case, but I can ask around."

Pinching his brows together, he glances over at me. "Jesus, Mara. No. No one's suing me for sexual harassment."

The car is silent for a couple very long minutes. Silence makes me uncomfortable, so I find a way to fill it.

"Carter and Suki got home. Hallie said she had fun."

He nods. "Carter looks like he's been on a month-long tropical getaway."

"Yeah, Suki had a little color, too. But she's so fair she doesn't really tan."

"You like Neptune's? For dinner?"

I've only been to the upscale restaurant once, when Carter and Suki invited me for dinner to celebrate Olivia's birthday. On my salary, the closest I get to seafood is usually a Filet-O-Fish.

"I don't care where we go. I'm good with bar food."

"Well, I'm buying, so we're going to Neptune's."

I look down at my fitted gray pants and black flats. With the red silky cami and black cardigan I'm also wearing, it's dressy enough, I suppose. On the rare occasions when I go to nice restaurants, I like to wear dresses and heels.

But this isn't a date. It's just a weird, impromptu dinner with Leo, whom I mostly dislike.

"Just tell me what it is," I blurt. "I can't stand not knowing."

"I want you to hear me out."

"And you think I won't do that if we're in the car?"

He shrugs a shoulder. "I think if you have a nice glass of wine on the way, you're less likely to blow up and leave."

"Okay." I shake my head, aggravated. "I can buy my own wine and drink it at home if I want to. Out with it."

He shifts in his seat, looking uncomfortable. "So it starts with my teammate Anson. He's a good guy, but he's hairier than a fucking gorilla. He's very masculine-looking, you know?"

"And this relates to me how?"

He sighs heavily. "He has a twin sister. And apparently she has a thing for me."

"Aw, she's blind?" I cover my mouth with my hand. "I'm sorry. That just slipped out."

He flicks a glare at me. "She's his twin sister, and she's coming here for New Year's Eve. He wants to fix me up with her, and when he mentioned it at dinner yesterday, I sort of told him I'm already seeing someone."

"There you go. Problem solved. No hurt feelings."

He nods, not saying anything. I just look at him for a few seconds, waiting.

"Are you going to get to the part where this has anything to do with me?"

"Just a sec ..." The light we're at turns green and he accelerates. "Just let me get up to a speed where you can't jump out of the car ... okay, surely this is fast enough. I, uh ... said I'm dating *you*."

CHAPTER NINE

Leo

MARA JUST GAPES at me for a couple of seconds. Then she laughs.

"Are you joking?"

I grip the steering wheel tighter, annoyed. "Why would I joke about this? It's not remotely funny."

Her smile slides away. "But why me? Aren't there like ... a thousand other women in your phone you could have asked?"

"It wasn't like that. It was a spur-of-the-moment thing, and Carter backed me up with the photo you took of us."

A note of laughter bursts out of her. "No, don't put this on me. I'm not part of your ... shenanigans just because of that photo."

"You don't have to actually date me. I just need you to go along with the story."

She pinches the bridge of her nose, not saying anything for a few seconds. When she finally speaks, she says, "It doesn't even make sense, Leo. Your team-mates have all seen us together at parties and they know it's all we can do not to strangle each other."

"We can tell them it took a turn. The passion was always there; we just rechanneled it."

She smiles, amused. "Rechanneled it?"

"Yeah. You're still yelling when we're together, but now you're yelling out my name while my face is between your thighs."

Her brows shoot up. "Really? Is this the charm that parts legs in every city you visit?"

"Not even close. You haven't seen any of the charm yet, but you will if you do this for me."

She furrows her brow in a half cringe. "I honestly don't think I can convince anyone I'm into you."

I bristle at that. "Why not? Am I really that bad?"

"No, you're actually very hot. But everyone knows we hate each other."

"You think I'm hot?"

Her cheeks flush with embarrassment. "I used to—before your drunken intrusion."

I have to force myself to focus on the road, though I'd rather look at her. Traffic is heavy, but within a minute, I'm pulling into the parking lot of Neptune's.

"Do you mind if I park in the lot next door? I'm kind of precious about my car."

"I'm precious about human rights. You and I are not the same. See what I mean?"

I ignore her jab and park my car in a spot without cars on either side of it.

"What can I say to convince you?" I ask on the walk into the restaurant.

"I can help you find someone for this. Easiest job ever with you being a hockey player. You'll be so much happier pretending to be with someone you could actually end up liking instead of me."

This is going about as well as I was worried it would. I run a hand through my hair, feeling a few cold snowflakes. "I already told him it's you, Mara. Can you please just do me this one favor?"

She stops walking, turning to me and lifting her chin so we're eye to eye. "Why would I do that? To be nice to you? I don't fucking care if you think I'm nice. I once heard you tell Carter I'm a spoiled brat whose voice makes you want to claw your own eyes out."

I exhale heavily, remembering the day I said that. I was in a shit mood. "That was more than a year ago."

"So fucking what? You still think that."

I pause, feeling the ruse slipping through my fingers. "Not as much. You stayed to help me with Darling—a brat wouldn't have done that."

"A brat." She crosses her arms, her eyes bright with anger. "You want to know how much of a brat I am, Leo? I'm two hundred eighty-one thousand dollars in debt from college and law school loans. I make sixty-eight thousand dollars a year and can barely afford my loan payments. If I'm wearing nice clothes or shoes, I bought them used. My parents have *nothing*."

Her voice breaks on the last word, and I feel like the world's biggest asshole.

"Mara, I'm—"

"I'm not done! My parents worked so fucking hard, Leo. So fucking hard, and everything was taken away from them for something they didn't deserve. I waitressed in high school just to keep food on the table when things were really bad with my dad. I promise you I am not the least bit spoiled, but you've never taken the time to know anything about me."

Angry tears well in her eyes. Or maybe they aren't angry. Her parents are clearly an emotional subject for her, and I didn't mean for us to get into something so heavy in the parking lot of Neptune's.

"I'm sorry," I say softly. "You're right. I made a stupid assumption and never bothered to find out the truth."

She looks away, the tears falling onto her cheeks when she blinks. "I don't want your pity. It's a lot easier when you're just an asshole."

"I don't pity you."

"Leo ... I have a lot of resentment inside me. A small sliver of it is toward you, but when I get mad, my resentment about other people and things can come flying out of me and hit whoever is closest. You'd have a hard time pretending to be into me, too."

"I shouldn't have asked. It was selfish."

She sighs, her exhale making a small cloud in the cold. "I'll do it for two hundred and fifty grand."

My chin drops in shock. "What?"

She turns to face me, vulnerability swirling in her caramel eyes as she holds my gaze. "For my parents. My dad was hit by a drunk driver when I was fourteen and he's paralyzed. I know it's a lot of money, but it would change their lives. I went to law school because I wanted to help them with money, but then I was an idiot who left my high-paying job to work in traffic court, so that's never happening."

It is a lot of money, but also, it's not. I've been smart with my money over the past ten years in pro hockey and I have more than twenty million dollars between savings and investments. Plus another two million in the bank that I can access anytime.

"Okay," I say.

Her eyes widen with shock. "Okay?"

I nod. "Yeah. You're right—if I'm getting something out of it, you should, too."

She opens her mouth, closes it, and then opens it again. "I ... wasn't expecting you to say that."

I nod at the restaurant, my hands freezing in the cold. "Let's talk about it over dinner."

"Okay, but before we even walk inside—I'm not sleeping with you." She's on the verge of tears again, and it hits me like a punch to the gut. "Not even for that much money."

I put my palms up. "I'd never ask you to do that. I'd never want any woman who didn't want me to do anything like that. This situation won't involve anything physical. Ever."

She wipes her fingertips beneath her eyes. "And you're still willing to do it? For that much money?"

The woman I call the queen of mean has her armor off in this moment, and I see how wrong I've been about her. She just wants to help her parents, and she's carrying around a lot of guilt over not being able to.

"You're the one doing me a favor." I fight my urge to reach out and cup her cheek, which is tinged pink from the cold.

"But this ... the money part, I mean ... can we not tell anyone? Suki knows about my parents, and Dex and Harry know a little bit, but not everything. I don't like talking about it."

I get that more than she'll ever know. I'm the same way about my brother's death. No matter how many years pass, it stays raw. Talking about it just reopens the wound.

"Just between us," I say. "I promise. You, me and my accountant will be the only ones who know, because she'll be the one sending the money."

She nods. "Thank you."

She turns to walk into the restaurant, and I follow. The lobby is crowded with people waiting for tables, but when I mention our team owner's name to the host, we're immediately led to a quiet table for two in the back of the restaurant.

"The fewer people who know the truth, the better,"

I say once we're in our seats and alone. "Especially on my team."

"Want me to post that selfie on my socials?"

Ugh. That's something I'll have to do, too. And when my friends and former teammates see it, I'll get flooded with messages. I've never posted a photo of a woman on my social media.

"Yeah," I say. "And send it to me. I'll post it too."

She gives me the devilish smile I know all too well. "Caption it, *My heart* and add a heart emoji."

I groan. "Come on. Everyone who knows me knows I'm not cheesy."

"You are for me." She rests her chin on her hand, grinning. "By the end of this, I'll have you posting about how you'd crawl through broken glass just to kiss my filthy, unmanicured feet."

I glare at her across the small table. "What's your handle? I have to follow you."

"I'm MaraTorres19 on all of them."

"What's the nineteen for?"

"My favorite constitutional amendment."

I roll my eyes. "Nerd."

"Caveman."

I pick up my menu. "Me hungry, so figure out what you want to order."

"I think we need pet names for each other."

I slump in my seat, dreading what she'll come up with.

"Mine should be about your ass, because obviously," she says.

I sit up straighter. "Obviously what?"

She lowers her brows. "You're going to make me say it? It's a great ass. There."

"You like my pro dumper?"

She wrinkles her nose. "Why did you just ruin it?"

"No, not like that. That's what we call a strong ass in hockey."

"I've noticed other guys on the team have decent asses, but yours is exceptional. Don't let it go to your head, though."

"You want me to sign a picture of it for you?"

She scoffs. "No."

"I should call you my little habanero."

Her jaw drops. "Fucking racist. I'm about to raise my price."

"I didn't mean it like that. I meant like because you're hot and spicy."

"Uh-huh. And I'll call you my little Neanderthal."

I focus on the menu, fighting my urge to keep escalating the argument. That's usually our style. We both want to get the last word in. But that's Mara all the time, and I'm not like that with anyone but her.

Conflict gives me anxiety--unless it's with her. Weirdly, I enjoy our interactions, even when she frustrates the hell out of me. It's kind of an outlet.

"We can easily get away without meeting each other's families because we can say things are still new," I say. "But I'll need you for some holiday stuff with my team. There's an ugly sweater party Wednesday evening. Can you make that?"

"Sure." She meets my gaze. "As long as I get to pick out your sweater."

I sigh softly. "Fine. You won't be able to shock my teammates. Better pick one fast, or it won't be here on time."

"It'll be fine. You can do expedited shipping."

I guess this is my life now. Playing hockey and amusing Mara. But it won't be forever. We can fake a hot and heavy relationship for a month and then say she dumped me and I'm devastated. That should buy me time with Anson.

And if nothing else, this year's holiday season will at least be memorable.

CHAPTER TEN

Mara

"THIS IS the saddest excuse for a lunch I've ever seen," Jayden mutters to me.

We're standing in the staff lounge for our office, and if I wasn't so hungry, the scene before me would be funny. For the holiday potluck, one person brought in a pan of cheesy potatoes, which are gone. Everyone else picked up trays of cookies from the store.

I pick up a hard chocolate chip cookie and take a small bite. "Well, we brought in cookies, so I guess we can't complain."

"I'm still complaining. After the morning I had, I think I'm entitled."

He did have a shitty morning. Someone bumped into him in the elevator and spilled coffee all over his dress shirt, and he didn't have an extra in his office, so he had to go to court in the wet one. The judge dressed him down for showing up looking like that, and then another judge dismissed the charges in a DUI case because the defendant's blood sample was mishandled.

It was a criminal case, so another attorney from our office was handling it, but we did some of the legwork on it. The defendant has served jail time for DUIs in the past, so it's likely he'll be out reoffending soon.

Bruce walks into the lounge and surveys the spread, shaking his head. "This is why we need a sign-up sheet."

"What did you bring?" I ask him.

He looks at me, his nostrils flaring. "Are you ready for our meeting?"

I nod, fighting my urge to smile. I work through lunch often, but the men in the office turn into hangry beasts when they don't get lunch.

Once we're in his office, Bruce opens a desk drawer and pulls out a bag of pretzels, then sits down in his squeaky chair. "Okay, did you review those cases?"

I sit down in a chair across from his desk. "Yes."

"What are your thoughts on the one that went down at Home Depot?"

"No deal. Plenty of witnesses and a victim willing to testify."

He nods. "What about *People v. McCoy*?"

"Is that the one where they both got arrested?"

"Yep."

"Plead it. He's remorseful and willing to go to rehab."

"Do you want to sit in on my meeting with his counsel?"

I stand up and walk to the corner of the room, ditching the rest of my cookie. "Yes. Just check my schedule and add it as long as I'm not in court."

"Will do. And *People v. Hadsell* is a bust because the victim won't testify."

"What?" I pull my brows together, my heart kicking up speed. "But he beat her unconscious."

Bruce shrugs. "I can't get a conviction without her testimony."

I close my eyes, the photos of the woman's injuries the police took at the hospital still fresh in my mind. Statistically, her abuser will keep hurting her, and it could be even worse next time.

"This is part of the job, Torres," Bruce says. "You can't win 'em all."

"Can I talk to her?"

I can tell he's about to say no, so I cut him off. "I'll be gentle, I promise. I'll mostly listen and if she's a hard no, I'll respect it. I just want a chance."

"She said no. That's it."

"But she could change her mind. She's pregnant, Bruce. Just one conversation, that's all I'm asking for. If nothing else, let me have one last conversation with her to let her know about the help that's available."

He chews a pretzel, considering. "One conversation. Don't make me regret it."

"You won't. Thank you."

He scowls at the bag of pretzels and rolls the top down, putting the bag back in his drawer. "I'm going to get lunch, you want to join me?"

"I have to pass, but thanks. I've got a thing tonight, so I need to get out of here a few minutes early."

He nods and stands up. "You know the drill. She comes here; you don't go to her home."

"Got it."

"I look forward to being bested by an attorney who wasn't even alive when I started practicing," he says wryly.

I panic for a second, but recover quickly. "It's not a contest. I just thought maybe having a woman closer to her age might help."

His lips curve up in a smile. "I'm messing with you, Torres. In this division, we take all the help we can get."

———

"I HOPE you're proud of yourself. My arms hurt."

Leo scowls at me that evening, his arms out at his sides like the kid in a snowsuit in *A Christmas Story*.

I really didn't intend to make him uncomfortable. When I bought the men's size small sweater-vest with one button and covered it with Christmas tree balls, I wanted him to look and feel ridiculous.

Instead, his very defined abs are on full display since the bottom of the vest is gaping open and he can't put his giant, muscular arms at his sides without breaking the balls. His tipsy teammates are still calling him "ballbuster" from the last time it happened a few minutes ago.

"Do you want me to take off some of them so you can put your arms down?" I ask.

"Some of what?"

I give him an *isn't it obvious* look. "The balls."

He arches his brows and grins. "You want to touch my balls? We haven't even been at this party an hour. Someone's frisky this evening."

"Offer rescinded." I take a sip of my wine, scanning the room for Suki.

When I find Suki, I see that she and Carter are talking to Anson and Lucien, and Anson is staring at me.

"Time for some insincere affection," I murmur, moving closer to Leo and looking up at him. "What would I be saying to you right now if we were together?"

His eyes are greener than any Christmas tree, something I don't recognize swirling in them.

"No one's ever fucked me the way you do, Leo," he says, his voice deeper and gruffer than usual. "I never should have doubted you. Can I practice my blow-job technique on you again tonight?"

I don't know if it's his words or the wine, but I laugh. His eyes shine with amusement and he says, "What? You don't think so? What would I be saying to you if we were together?"

I consider for a second. "Probably something like,

91

Mara, you're the smartest woman I've ever known. What charities do you support that I can write big checks to so I can, in some small way, make up for walking in on you in the bathroom?"

He holds my gaze, still smiling. "Like a desperate pervert."

It's what I called him in the heat of the moment that day, when I was panicking about him seeing me naked. But something about the way he just said the words is making my heart feel fluttery.

"The most desperate pervert I've ever known."

It's all I can do to get the words out, because Leo's giving me the *I'm about to kiss you* look. And for some reason I can't explain, I want him to. Is it my long-term lack of physical affection? The spirit of the holiday season? Whatever it is, I'm not a fan.

I clear my throat, ending the moment. "I need to go talk to Suki." I pass him my wineglass. "Would you mind getting me a refill?"

He takes the glass. "You want anything to eat?"

"Mm, I'm good for now. I like to get my buzz on and then eat."

"As you wish."

I watch him go as he walks over to the bar, admiring his "pro dumper." He's built for long nights of endless positions in bed. But just because he has a body that makes me salivate, that doesn't mean he knows how to use it. He could be one of those guys who jackhammer women into oblivion and rubs their clits like he's trying to remove a carpet stain.

That has to be Leo. Suki has told me he's what they call a grinder in hockey, because he gives a hundred and ten percent all day, every day. He doesn't score a lot, but he does whatever it takes to create opportunities for his teammates to. I'm sure he's the same in the bedroom, grinding his partners into the mattress.

"Need this?"

I turn to find Suki standing next to me, holding out a napkin.

"No, why?" I say, confused.

"I thought you might want to wipe away your drool."

I roll my eyes. "Oh, please. I can admire the packaging without wanting to unwrap it."

"Uh-huh. Either you two missed your calling as actors, or there's something there. I saw the way you were looking at each other."

"Pfft." I take a sip of my wine. "Only because you know who was looking at us. We were talking about how much we hate each other."

"Oh, I'm sure."

I give her a sympathetic look. "I know you think you've got this all figured out and you're mentally picking out your matron of honor dress already, but babe, Leo and I are like fetch. We're never going to happen."

"Because why would you want a guy who rescues freezing puppies? While also having those abs?" She sips her wine. "Where's your glass, by the way?"

I don't even realize I'm scanning the people in the

room, looking for Leo, until my gaze lands on him. There's a woman talking to him in the drink line, and she's laughing. Though his washboard abs are out of view since his side is facing me, I can still appreciate the cut muscles in his thick upper arms.

"Leo's getting me another one."

Suki balks, throwing her head back slightly. "And he gets you drinks?"

I roll my eyes. "You know the situation. We're playing at being a couple. He has to do things like that."

"Does that mean you'll be hanging onto his arm later and looking at him adoringly?" She smirks.

"Um, no. I'm here, and that's me holding up my end of the bargain."

"It is really nice of you to do this for him. It reminds me of me and Carter." She furrows her brow, speaking in a low tone. "I can't believe Leo wore that when he's supposed to be happily dating someone. He looks like he's on the prowl with his muscles on display like that."

"I picked it out," I admit.

Her eyes bulge and she laughs lightly. "I see. Just know that as your best friend, I'm entitled to at least a text within twenty-four hours of you clawing up his back for the first time."

"Fetch, remember?"

Leo is talking to a man I don't know now, and his back is facing me. The small sweater-vest is stretched across his broad back, light hitting some of the shining ball ornaments. I mentally file away a quip about him

94

having a lot of balls for once, knowing I'll find a time to use it at some point tonight.

I still can't believe I told him about my dad. Nothing and no one means more to me than my parents, and I safeguard their vulnerability with my whole being. Probably because it's also my own vulnerability. They live in Indianapolis, where my mom's sister also lives. Aunt Rhonda is a big source of emotional support to my mom, and she helps with my dad's care.

On our weekly FaceTime calls, my parents' faces glow as I tell them about my work. Even though I just handle speeding tickets and other mundane cases, they think I'm a rock star prosecutor. They've been adamant since I left for college that they want me to live my life. They don't want me to be a caregiver to my dad. He told me during my senior year of high school that the greatest gift I could give him would be to truly leave home and chase my dreams.

I usually make it home every six to eight weeks for a quick visit, but I still feel guilty I'm not there more. I thought when I started law school that I'd at least have the money to change their lives, but then I had to work on a case at my first law firm that went against everything I believe in.

And still, they're proud of me. I'm an only child, and I don't know if I'll ever give them grandchildren. They've told me to do what makes me happy.

Being able to send them two hundred and fifty

thousand dollars is going to make me ridiculously happy. They might even be able to afford to move into a home that's fully accessible for my dad. They had to make the living room of their small two-story home into a bedroom after the accident because my dad couldn't get upstairs.

"Mara?"

I snap out of my daze, looking at Suki. "Sorry, what?"

She shakes her head, a smile tugging on her lips. "You were off in your own world, staring at the guy you can't stand."

I wave a hand, dismissing her. "I wasn't even thinking about him."

"Right."

I can tell she doesn't believe me, but I drop it. Leo is walking back toward us now, a woman he passes gaping at his sweater-vest. But really, she's gaping at his body.

And how can she not? That single button is fighting for its life, looking like it could fly off at any moment. I should have gotten him a frumpy turtleneck sweater.

Live and learn, I guess. I'll be spending this entire evening with Leo and his abs, so my second glass of wine will be my last.

It's not just his body, but those mossy-green eyes and his playful smirk, that could make me forget reason and ask him to come home with me.

God, would that be fun. I lick my lips just thinking about it.

It's a terrible idea, though. The worst. I'm not here to see Leo in a different light and change my mind about him. I'm here for the money my parents are going to get.

Even though there's good wine and I'm feeling more than a little bit merry, this is just a transaction.

CHAPTER ELEVEN

Leo

THE RICH, savory scent of Suki's cheese fondue makes my stomach grumble with hunger.

I follow Carter into the kitchen, say quick greetings to Suki, Charlotte, and Dex, and then grab a hunk of bread and dip it into the fondue fountain.

Once I pop it into my mouth, I groan with satisfaction. Suki's monthly fondue night is better than a lot of holidays.

"Whoa. What is that?"

A teenage girl I don't recognize approaches the fondue fountain with Olivia. Must be one of her friends.

"It's cheese fondue," Olivia says. "Suki made it."

"Hey, Liv." I smile at the girls.

"Hi, Uncle Leo. This is my friend Macy."

"Nice to meet you, Macy."

"Thanks, you too."

Carter has told me and Bash about Olivia's volatile teenage moods, and I don't envy him having to navigate them. She's not around as much when I'm over, but she gets good grades and keeps out of trouble, so I assume she's just busy with friends. I know I felt awkward as fuck at her age.

I let the girls have full access to the cheese and chocolate fondue fountains. Carter and Dex are sitting together, both eating, when I sit down next to Carter in the dining room.

"Hey, Leo," Dex says. "Where's your faux beau?"

"No idea. We haven't talked since she went to a team party with me a few days ago."

"What a game last night. You guys smashed it."

Carter's brows rise. "You watched it, Dex?"

"I did. I added a hockey all-access package to my obnoxiously expensive cable plan. I'm a Crush fan, of course, but between us, did you guys hire those refs last night or what? They're probably still scrubbing shit out of their hair from having their entire heads up your coach's ass."

I scoff. "Not every call is right, but it all evens out. You win some, you lose some."

Dex sets down his celery stick. "No. Lucien should have been called for boarding. Twice. The ref was looking right at him."

Carter shrugs a shoulder. "I saw one time he should've been called. But it was John McMahon getting boarded, and that guy's a massive douchebag, so fuck it. And when you win 6–2, a few different calls wouldn't have changed the outcome."

"You've really gotten into the game," I say to Dex.

He shrugs. "Suki makes us watch games when we're over and they're on, and it's really grown on me. I was on a business trip recently and I was *that guy*, asking the bartender at the airport bar to change the channel so I could catch part of a hockey game."

"Leo, hi," Suki says, coming into the dining room and giving me a quick arm around the shoulder hug. "Aren't you going to eat?"

"Yeah, I was letting the kids go first."

Darling follows her into the room, his tail swishing when he sees me.

"There he is," I say, putting my hand out. "Come get your head scratches, big guy."

He loves having his head, ears and back scratched and rubbed. When Mara and I were taking care of him, she'd absently rub his back for a solid hour at a time, scrolling her phone with the other hand.

"Where's everyone else?" I ask Suki.

"Harry had to work, Lainey and Bash will be here later, and I don't know about Mara. She bought some cookies from someone at the courthouse who has a side business, and she was planning to bring them. But she texted and said she didn't know if she would make it."

I feel a twinge of disappointment. We had a nice time at the party, and I left for a quick road trip the morning after. More than once, I thought about her smile when I changed into the sweater-vest she got me. Her sudden grin was bright and warm and so damn happy, and it was directed entirely at me.

I've seen her smile that way at Suki before. But when Mara looks at me, her shoulders usually slump with disappointment. I get glares and eye rolls. Sarcastic laughter. I liked her sincere, light expression when I stepped out of my car, where I changed into the vest.

We drove separately to the party, so we just said a quick goodbye at the end. Anson had already left, so there was no need to fake a kiss.

I was hoping to see her tonight. There's one more team holiday event I'll need her to be my date to, and then the New Year's Eve thing. I'll have to text her the dates and times.

Lainey and Bash come, and after I say hi to them, I make myself a plate of bread, meat, veggies and fondue. About to head back to the dining room, I hear someone come in the door that leads from the garage into the kitchen.

It's Mara. Her eyes are red, the skin around them puffy, and she's holding a white box in her hands. She puts a finger to her lips and whispers softly.

"I just want to drop these sugar cookies off and go."

"What's wrong?" I ask, keeping my voice low.

She presses her lips together, her expression pained. "Horrible day at work. It was either stay home and eat this entire box myself or drop them off. I can't people right now."

Everyone has bad days at work. When I get home from road trips, I usually can't wait to get home to my quiet house. My anxiety can be exhausting, and time alone helps me get out of my own head.

I should let Mara slip out and go home to recharge, but something makes me set my plate down.

"I'm fine," she says.

"I'll walk you out," I offer.

"You don't have to."

I ignore her, opening the door to the garage. She sighs heavily, hikes the strap of her bag over her shoulder, and walks out the door.

"I'm okay, really." She turns to me once I've closed the door. "I just don't want to have to explain why I look like hell. I want to crawl into bed and be alone."

"You sure?" I cross my arms over my chest, concerned. "I could hang out and watch a show with you. I won't talk."

She shakes her head, and my worry grows deeper. I've never seen Mara like this. Everything about her expression says she's defeated.

"It's just work?" I ask.

"Yeah. I fucked up. I'm sure you'd love to hear all about it." Her tone is biting, and she cringes as soon as the words are out of her mouth. "I'm sorry. I just want to rage, and that's why I shouldn't be around anyone right now."

Carter's giant garage is a weird place to be having

this conversation. His big SUV and Suki's smaller one are parked inside the space, but there's still lots of open room.

"You can rage at me," I say. "I can take it."

"Don't, Leo," she snaps. "Not right now."

"Let it out. It's not good to hold everything in."

She sneers at me. "Are you my shrink now? I told you to leave me alone, so leave me the fuck alone."

I'd usually respect that request, but somehow I know if I don't push her, Mara will go home and marinate in her feelings of failure. Probably because I do it myself. Anxiety and depression can turn a tiny snowball into an avalanche.

"Did you get fired?" I ask her.

"No, I didn't get fired. I'm just fucking hungry and exhausted and completely fucking—" She looks away, unable to finish. "I can't do this, Leo."

I can't get over how absolutely broken she looks. It's so unlike her—Mara is usually proud and steely, her resolve never showing so much as a crack.

"You're human, you know," I say. "You get to make mistakes."

She shakes her head. "You don't get it. My job is a lot different than yours. I'm not playing a game."

I keep pushing. "Did some kids refuse to drink the potion you brewed? Did they not cry when you cackled at them?"

Her nostrils flare with aggravation. "I'm really not in the mood for your bullshit, Leo."

"So tell me what happened and we can drop it."

She pinches the bridge of her nose. "When have you ever dropped anything? You'll be making fun of my bush at my damn funeral."

I bark a note of laughter. "Me? You carry a grudge like no one I've ever seen."

Her voice rises as she says, "Fuck you, Leo. Only you would kick me when I'm already down. This is why I can't stand you."

Tears shine in her eyes. I should listen to her and leave her alone, but I push her further instead.

"It's probably not even a big deal. Are you just being melodramatic?"

She bursts open like a dam, her eyes darkening with rage. "Not a big deal? Kiss my entire ass, Leo! I need a woman to testify against her abuser, and I tried to convince her, but she won't. She's back with him! He'll hurt her worse next time. He might even kill her. Because I couldn't do my job."

Tears stream down her cheeks, and my heart cracks. She's usually prickly and defensive, and talk about a hothead, but Mara's passion runs both ways. When she wants something, she fights for it.

"It's not your fault," I say, putting a hand on the side of her shoulder.

She crumbles, burying her face in her hands. "I thought I could do it. I'm so stupid. When I told her"— her voice breaks with a sob— "to think of her baby, she got mad. She wouldn't even—"

I bristle with anger. "Fuck."

Quickly closing the distance between us, I put my

arms around her. She resists for a second before going limp in my arms, crying harder now.

"You can't blame yourself."

She just cries for a full minute, then presses her palms to my chest and pushes herself back several inches, looking up at me. "I don't know if I can do this job. And I couldn't do the last one either, so ..." She laughs sadly. "Guess I'm fucked."

"Of course you can do this job. They're damn lucky to have you."

She shakes her head, fresh tears pooling in her eyes. "Look at me. I'm not supposed to be a mess over something like this."

"It's because you care. A lot better you than some suit who doesn't give a shit."

She looks away. "I was taking a soft approach, but you know me. I'm about as soft as a battle-ax."

That makes me smile. "Yeah, but how effective would a feather battle-ax be? You have to be tough to prosecute criminals."

She *almost* smiles. It's something. "I work in traffic court, Leo. My cases aren't even felonies."

"Then what were you doing talking to this woman today?"

"My boss is having me learn a little bit about domestics. Those are felonies."

"You must be doing a good job with the traffic stuff, then."

She sighs heavily. "I wanted to convince her so fucking bad. I wanted to help her so she could have her baby in a safe place and break the cycle of violence."

"She has to choose it for herself. You offered her a hand, but it's up to her whether or not to take it."

"There's no case without her." She looks miserable. "He just walks free and gets to do it again."

Though my job doesn't compare to hers because of the real-world stakes in a case like this, I offer her the advice Dr. Laudner has given me for dealing with a shitty performance in a game.

"Think of an amount of time you're going to let yourself feel bad about this. After that, move forward."

She exhales heavily. "I guess tonight. Until I fall asleep. I'm out of wine, so I can't drown my sorrows."

"You sure you don't want to come in?"

She furrows her brow. "No. Suki will want to talk about it and tell me I'm amazing, and I don't want to hear it. She means well, but ... not tonight."

"Is there anything I can do?"

"Just cover for me with Suki."

"Hey." I wait for her eyes to lock onto mine. "You didn't fuck anything up. She's just not ready."

She steps back, one of her palms lingering on my chest. "I know. I'll be a battle-ax again tomorrow."

"You okay to drive?"

She nods, dropping her hand. "I'm good. I'm getting a drive-through burrito and putting on my pajamas the second I walk into my apartment."

"Text me to let me know you made it home okay."

"Okay."

There's a spark of warmth in her eyes, and she almost smiles. Then she turns to leave, entering the code to close the garage door at the keypad next to one of the doors.

The door closes, blocking her from my view. But just like when I was on my road trip, I'm still thinking about her, even when I can't see her.

CHAPTER TWELVE

Mara

I REALLY NEED to eat a vegetable every now and then. Unless salsa counts, I'm fucked on veggie consumption.

Coffee, wine, Taco Tony's drive-through burritos and turkey sandwiches from the deli near the courthouse make up most of my diet. And the seat of the used Peloton I was so excited about picking up on Marketplace last year has a thick layer of dust on it.

Curling up on my couch with my phone and a fuzzy blanket, I turn on Netflix, not paying close attention to the show I resume.

Law school was stressful, but it was a different kind of stress. I worked part-time jobs and studied a lot, so keeping my bills paid and doing well in school were my main worries.

My first job out of law school was also stressful,

mostly due to the hours. A twelve-hour day was considered light, and I'd usually have work to catch up on at home, too. It was a cutthroat culture where billable hours meant more than anything and no one cared who they had to step on to win or move up.

I send my mom a text, telling her work is good and I'm seeing someone. Neither of those things is true, but I don't want her to know the truth. Surprisingly, Leo made me feel a lot better.

Suki would have hovered and insisted we talk it to death. Talking about it at length would have made me feel worse. I need time and space.

Leo caused me to boil over, but I actually felt better afterward. Like a steam valve had been turned to lessen the pressure inside me. Now I just feel heavy and weary.

When I saw Libby Harn, I thought I'd be able to get through to her. I overestimated myself, I guess. Figured a woman-to-woman talk would help her see things more clearly. But I was wrong. She got angry at me and accused me of judging her. I think that hurt more than her refusal to testify did, because it's true.

I do judge her for staying, and I don't like myself for it. I took a class on domestic abuse and learned about the many layers of manipulation it often involves. Some men are even able to convince their victims that they hurt them *because* they love them.

It's sick. I thought my toughness would help me shatter generational cycles of abuse in cases like this, but instead, I have to accept that I can't win every case.

I can't convince every victim to testify. I'll eventually lose criminal trials that mean a lot to me.

I left the law firm about a year into my job there because of a case I was assigned to. A partner was handling it, but I was assisting. Our client was a big insurance company that had denied coverage to a baby who needed corrective surgery for its mouth so it could latch on and eat. The insurance company said the condition was preexisting because the baby was born with it. The parents had to sell their home immediately, below market value, to secure enough money for the hospital to agree to perform the surgery.

I sat through one meeting with representatives of the insurance company, packed my few personal belongings into a box when it was over and resigned.

Fuck that. My parents lost everything because of what happened to my dad. I'll go back to waitressing before I help an insurance company fuck innocent people over.

My eyelids are getting heavy, the day catching up with me, when my phone buzzes with a text.

Mom: You're seeing someone? What's his name? How many dates have you been on?

I'll have to disappoint her when I eventually tell her it didn't work out, but I might as well give my mom some false hope. It won't hurt anything, and it'll make her happy.

Mara: His name is Leo and he's a hockey player on the team Suki's husband Carter is on. We've known each other for a while. Just a couple of dates so far.

Mom: Tell me more! How old is he? Is he Catholic?

I smile at the screen. My parents are devout Catholics. Even though they can't attend church easily in person, they watch services on television. I have to turn on my profanity filter when I go home, because they'd lose their minds if they knew how many f-bombs I drop every day.

I'm not even sure how old Leo is, so I make up a number.

Mara: He's thirty, and I don't know if he's Catholic.

Mom: How can you not know? You haven't talked about your religion with him?

I evade the question by sending her the prank selfie and another photo of us at the ugly sweater party. She's not on social media, so she wouldn't have seen them when I posted them.

Mom: Oh honey, he's so handsome! So tall! You make a beautiful couple. But why is he wearing that sweater vest that's too small for him?

I can almost hear her voice, which helps soothe my aching heart. My mom is everything I'm not: sweet, nurturing and kind. Even with everything she's been through, she's never faltered.

Mara: I think it looks good on him.

Mom: I just don't understand why he didn't want a sweater that fits him. It's winter.

I change the subject.

Mara: How's Dad?

Mom: He's good. We're excited about seeing you for Christmas. Will Leo be joining you?

My stomach flips nervously at the thought of Leo meeting my parents. It's too much. Suki has met them, but she's my best friend. I don't want Leo seeing the filtered side of me I reserve for my family.

It would get their hopes up too much. Dad already watches every Cleveland Crush game because Suki's husband is on the team. I couldn't handle getting pictures of him in a Crush hat, celebrating Leo's goals.

I wish I could give my parents that kind of happiness, but I'm not much on relationships. I know I've got sharp edges and I'm a lot, and I'm okay with it. I don't need a man trying to tame me into his ideal partner.

Mara: No. It's not serious or anything. We've only been on a couple of dates.

Mom: I don't understand kids these days. Vicki's daughter has been "hanging out" with a man for more than six months now. What does that even mean? Your father and I were engaged five months after we started dating.

I'm fighting sleep. I can't wait to put this day behind me, so I end the conversation with my mom.

Mara: I'm going to bed, Mom. Love you. Tell Dad I love him too.

Mom: I will. We love you.

I get up from the couch and walk into my kitchen, looking at a photo of me and Suki on the front of the fridge. With only the dim glow of the microwave light illuminating the room, I can't see much, but I can see our smiles. The picture was taken after we did a charity mud run together, and we're both caked in mud.

Suki and I used to share this apartment, and I need to give it up and move somewhere smaller and more affordable since it's just me and I don't have a six-figure salary anymore. I've dragged my feet on it because I have good memories of us here.

She's moved on to the stage of life she always dreamed of reaching: marriage and kids. A beautiful home. Hosting friends and family. She was made for all of it.

What am I made for? I thought I knew, but now I'm not so sure. I saw myself slaying in corporate law. Putting in endless hours and making a name for myself. Getting myself and my parents out of debt. Traveling. Volunteering for causes I believe in.

The grind of law school was supposed to be the end of my struggle. Instead, I'm just drifting. I don't have a direction. I like my job and I love my friends, but at the end of every day, I'm alone.

Maybe I need a pet or something. Dex is happily single. We've talked about living together, but it wouldn't work. He's a neat freak whose dishes all face the same direction. I like my home to feel lived in, with blankets and pillows on the couches and chairs and books and plants stacked on every empty surface. We'd drive each other crazy.

It feels good to crawl into my bed and burrow beneath the warm covers. I'm setting an alarm on my phone for morning when a photo text comes in from Leo.

It's a meme that says, "When you find a serious leek

under your sink." There's a stalk of leek beneath a kitchen sink with a frowning face drawn on the vegetable in marker.

Leo: Tomorrow will be better.

There's a slight burn in my eyes. I already know I'm done hating him. He judged me without knowing me well, and I did the same thing to him.

I needed a friend after my horrible day at work, but I didn't even realize it. His hug and words of wisdom took a weight off my shoulders.

Even though I knew I'd tried my best with Libby, I still felt guilty. And humbled. I was so arrogant that I really thought I could accomplish something Bruce couldn't.

Leo said exactly what I needed to hear, and then he gave me the space I needed. He understood how I felt. I'm embarrassed about all the times I've insinuated—or even outright said—that he's not smart. Called him a caveman. Said he's the emotional equivalent of a black hole.

I say I'm too much for some people, but I feel like too much even for myself right now. I hope he's right and tomorrow will be better.

I text him back.

Mara: Thanks. Want me to come to your game tomorrow night with Suki?

Leo: If you feel like it, sure.

Mara: I will.

Leo: Okay, see you after. Goodnight.

Mara: Night.

CHAPTER THIRTEEN

Leo

"WHY IS THE FUCKING BENCH WET?" I gripe, wiping it off with a towel.

"Might be shit," Carter mutters. "This whole bench smells like a frat house toilet."

We just came back to the bench after a line change, and I'm gassed. It was a long shift of nonstop skating up and down the ice. I'm breathing hard when I finally sit down.

"It's you, isn't it?" Carter's leaning forward, talking to Lucien, who's a couple guys to my right.

"It's fucking Bash." Lucien says. "It's always Bash."

Carter looks at Bash, who's sitting on his other side.

"It's that Alfredo sauce," Bash says. "Why do we have Alfredo sauce before a game?"

Carter shakes his head. "It's not the chef's fault

you're ripping so much ass, there's probably a hole in the ass of your pants."

"I can't help it."

Our second offensive line is killing it tonight. They've scored both goals we have on the board so far. Jack Grover fires a puck at the net and I lean forward, willing it to go in.

"Nice, Grover!" I yell.

It brushes against the edge of the net, but misses. I groan in disappointment, along with most of the fans in the arena.

When I see Grover skating toward the bench, I get up, positioning myself to replace him as quickly as I can. As soon as he's close enough, I move from the wall onto the ice, digging my skate blades in hard to help me catch up.

I'm pretty sure Mara's here. Carter said Suki told him she was coming. I resisted my urge to text her all day, making myself focus on my game-day routine instead.

Her tortured expression yesterday really got me. I've called her icy and void of emotions many times, but she's really the opposite. She feels a lot. Though she tries to make it look like nothing gets to her, she feels like a failure sometimes. Same as me.

When play stops, I look up at Carter's season ticket seats. I can barely make out Mara's dark hair beside Suki. Suki and the girls sometimes watch from one of the boxes, but they prefer to watch games from the stands, where they're closer to the action.

Something about trying to make Mara feel better yesterday made me feel more grounded today. I kept myself in my routine, but stayed ready in case she texted that her day wasn't any better. I even thought about how I'd respond.

People don't usually come to me for comfort or advice. Carter is our team captain, and if someone on our team needs guidance on something, whether it's hockey or just life, he's the one they go to.

Bash is a lighthearted extrovert who would listen if someone needed him to. He can be serious when he needs to be.

I'm more of a loner. I love my teammates and they're like my family, but I never let anyone see too much of the real me. I hardly ever have anyone over because I don't want people getting an up-close view of me.

My meds sit on my kitchen counter. A bookshelf in my living room has lots of sci-fi and history books, but also self-help ones. Books about anxiety and depression that Dr. Laudner has recommended. My home is the only place I can completely let my guard down, so I don't hide the things I don't want other people to see. I just don't invite anyone over.

Carter and Bash are on the ice with me now, and we fall into our rhythm of passing. No more thinking about Mara; I have to focus completely on the game.

One of Toronto's defenders slams into me and I hit the boards, pain lancing through my knee when it gets turned sharply and suddenly. I elbow him and recover, getting away quickly.

Skating fast and well has been drilled into me since I was a kid. My youth hockey coach emphasized skating fundamentals above anything else, and I'm a better player for it. He used to tell us we wouldn't be able to make a basket or hit a home run on ice skates unless we had mastered skating first, and hockey is no different.

I wouldn't have made it this far without my skating speed and skills. I still drill on it all the time, my trainer timing me and helping me stay fit enough to keep my times from slipping.

An unexpected opening comes and I take it, firing a slap shot that sends the puck into the net. The arena erupts with cheers, horns and music, my teammates gathering around me.

"There you go, man," Anson says with a grin.

He really is a nice guy. Faking a relationship with Mara was the best way to avoid dating his sister without offending him. He hasn't brought his sister up at all since I told him about Mara.

It's not a long-term solution, but it's getting me by for now. And for two hundred and fifty thousand dollars, I'm sure Mara will be willing to show up at events with me now and then for a while.

"Teaching them kids how it's done!" Andrei says when I return to the bench, clapping me on the knee.

I just nod in response because my knee hurts like a

bitch. Usually I get sudden, sharp pain that goes away quickly, but it's not going away this time.

And even worse, I have to keep playing like nothing's wrong. I think I'm doing a good job of hiding it. But as soon as we get back to the locker room, the mood light because we won 4–1, our head trainer Marina approaches me.

"What's up with your left knee?" she asks me.

I shrug. "Just tweaked it. It's fine."

"I want to look at it."

Fuck. That's going to be excruciating. She'll do a bunch of range of motion shit and I won't be able to hide the pain completely.

"Okay, I'll find you in a little bit."

She leaves, and I try to think of a way out of it. My pulse pounds as I strip off my gear, my chest aching faintly. There's a one-hundred-percent chance that if I let her examine my knee, she'll find out I have a torn meniscus, which will not only mean I have an anxiety attack in the locker room for the second time, but also that I'll get benched.

Caroline covered for me last time, so no one knew I had an anxiety attack. But I don't think I'll get that lucky a second time.

And being benched will be even worse. I'll get put on rest and I might even have to get surgery. If I'm not pushing myself hard in workouts, practices, and games every day, I'll lose my edge. I'll get slower. And I might not be able to get back to where I am.

I can barely hold my shit together now. If I lose my career, especially if it's because I try to return and let my team down by not being the same player anymore ...

The pain in my chest gets sharper. I breathe in and out, then head for the shower. I wash myself quickly, trying to breathe through the increasing ache in my chest.

It's not a heart attack. It's just anxiety. You have medication for this.

My knee is killing me. I just want to go home and sit on my couch with Birdie. The dog sitter I hired spent a few hours with her today since I had to be gone all day and night, so I know she's okay. I want to sit with her because I need it, not because she does.

I already can't imagine life without her waiting for me at the door every time I get home. We go on walks and I've started jogging with her. She doesn't like being outside without me, probably because she was abandoned in the freezing cold.

I committed to going out with some teammates after the game, though. If it was just me, I'd tell Carter I'm skipping it, but Mara's going.

I'm lightheaded. Between my chest and my knee, it's all I can do to put on a happy face when I leave the locker room.

"Hey Abbott, great game," Dana, a security guard, calls out.

"Thanks."

I duck my head and take the fastest route I can to the parking lot. Once I'm alone in my car, I put both hands on my steering wheel and rest my forehead on my hands, taking a few deep breaths.

Though I escaped Marina tonight, she'll find me tomorrow and force me into an exam. Getting out of there was supposed to make me feel better, but my chest pain is getting worse.

Fuck. What if it is a heart attack this time?

I have medication for anxiety attacks at home. I need to convince Mara to leave this dinner as quickly as possible so I can get home and get some medication in me.

That's going to be easier said than done—especially when they'll have wine at the restaurant. She usually doesn't eat much, if anything, before dinner, so she'll want to eat and drink.

I can't wait that long, though. I send her a text.

Leo: When you get to the restaurant, pull me aside. Pretend it's so you can privately congratulate me on my game.

Deep breaths aren't helping much. I open the calming sounds app on my phone and turn up the volume; the sound of a babbling brook and chirping birds comes on.

The restaurant is close. We'll make an appearance and get the hell out of there.

I rub my chest as I drive, shaking my head.

Fuck. Why didn't I just tell Anson I'm not interested in dating his sister?

CHAPTER FOURTEEN

Mara

I READ the text from Leo again, my concern growing. Usually I tell Suki everything, but I didn't tell her about his message.

Leo covered for me last night, and it was exactly what I needed. In the moment, I was devastated about not convincing Libby to testify, but I woke up feeling more clearheaded this morning.

That disappointment is part of my job. I needed to let myself fall apart since I'm new to it, but then I had to put it aside and move on. Maybe she'll think about the things I said and change her mind. I hope so.

Leo probably just wants to get our stories lined up since Anson will be at dinner tonight. It's probably just something small, and I'm worried for nothing.

Suki, beside me in the driver's seat, glances at her rearview mirror.

"Hey girls, I've been meaning to ask, does anyone know where the cocoa powder is? I was baking yesterday and I couldn't find it. I know I have some."

"No idea," Charlotte says absently.

Olivia is in the SUV's third row, probably listening to music on her headphones. The youngest girl, Hallie, pipes up.

"Maybe someone hid it under my bed."

Suki furrows her brow. "That's oddly specific, Hals."

"I'm just saying maybe."

"Okay."

I suppress a smile. Hallie cracks me up often without even trying.

"I've always wondered what baking cocoa tastes like by itself," I say, giving Suki a knowing look.

"*Not* like chocolate," Hallie says. "It's really bad. Don't make chocolate milk with it."

Suki sighs softly and we exchange an amused look. I shrug.

"It looks just like hot cocoa mix," I say in Hallie's defense before changing the subject. "How's Darling?"

"Good. He fell asleep on me and I couldn't move because his head is heavy."

I didn't think I wanted kids before Suki married Carter and his nieces became like daughters to her. I'm not so sure anymore, though. I love the girls and really do feel like an aunt to them. I see what Suki has with her family and think maybe someday I want that, too.

It's a school night, so we drop the girls off at home before going to the restaurant. They don't get to attend many games on school nights, but tonight they did. The babysitter Suki hired meets us in the garage to herd the girls into the house.

"Bring home some breadsticks," Charlotte says to Suki, adding, "Please."

"Got it. With extra cheese dip," Suki says.

She backs out of the garage and closes the door, glancing over at me.

"Carter is so ready for a baby. I keep putting him off because I'm waiting for you and Leo to make this thing official, so we can get pregnant at the same time."

I cringe. "Don't say it like that, gross. It makes me feel like we'll be side by side on our backs getting railed."

"What's wrong with you? You know what I meant."

"Leo and I will probably come out of this fake relationship as friends," I admit. "But we're definitely not getting married. Have your baby, and then if I have one in a few years, your kid can babysit my kid."

She groans. "That's not as fun."

I yawn, my early morning and late night catching up with me. "How long will this thing be? I have to get up for work in the morning."

"Not super late. The guys are leaving early tomorrow for a road trip."

"Okay, good. Eating carbs is going to knock my ass out."

Suki got me a jersey—or I guess, a sweater, as

127

hockey players apparently call them—with Leo's last name on the back. I'm wearing it even though it's not really my thing. It's comfortable, and I do love a night out in black leggings and tennis shoes.

When we get to the restaurant, several players are already at the table. One of them is Anson, who gives me a tight-lipped nod in greeting.

Leo's eyes lock onto me as I make sure to say hi to everyone at the table. When I turn my gaze to his, my concern comes back. I can tell from his expression that something is wrong. I turn on the charm so I can get him alone.

"Hey babe, can I talk to you?" I give him an adoring smile, biting my lip for good measure.

"Yeah, of course."

He slides his chair out and stands, taking my hand and leading me toward the restaurant's entrance. I give his hand a gentle, reassuring squeeze as we pass tables full of people. Some of them look at him as we pass, and I hear someone murmur, "Cleveland Crush."

Stopping in the lobby of the restaurant, he glances over at our table, which is still in full view.

"We can go outside if you want," I murmur.

"No, it needs to be here. Follow my lead."

We're facing each other, only about a foot of space between us. He puts his hands on my hips and I stop breathing. In his dark, perfectly cut suit, he could easily pass for a model or an actor. He looks polished and completely in control, my heart racing with awareness as I wrap my arms around his neck.

He rests his forehead lightly on mine and speaks softly, his words barely a whisper.

"I need you to pretend like you're desperate to get me home. I have to get out of here, but I don't want Anson to think there's anything wrong between us."

His voice is anything but in control. He sounds almost anguished, his hold on my hips firm.

"What's going on?" I ask.

He exhales through his nose. "It's nothing. We're going to pretend we're leaving together and I'll call you an Uber. Will you just please do this for me?"

"You're going to hook up with someone, aren't you?"

It shouldn't hurt, but it does. I just spent more than four hours at his game, meeting people and pretending to be his adoring girlfriend, and he can't even sit through dinner with me?

"No." He closes his eyes and cringes, looking like he's in pain. "Please, Mara. I covered for you, now I need you to cover for me."

The pleading in his tone tugs at my heart. "Okay. I'm going to lay on the affection. Give it like fifteen seconds and then act like you're reluctantly stopping me."

I don't even wait for him to answer before I move my fingers up his neck and into his hair, smiling. I press myself against him and barely brush my lips over his.

His body is like a brick wall. I've never been with a man so tall or so fit, and for a second, I wish I really was going home with him for a horizontal celebration of his win.

This close, I can smell the faint pine scent of his bodywash and feel the movement of his chest as he breathes faster than I am.

"How's this for convincing, desperate pervert?" I say lightly against his mouth.

I feel his lips quirking with a smile. "It's damn good."

His expression is reluctant as he pulls away and takes my hand.

"That actually helped," he says, looking surprised.

"Helped what?"

Ignoring my question, he leads me back to the table, where he announces, "We're passing on dinner, guys. My girl's hungry for something else and she wants to use every hour we've got until the plane takes off for the road trip."

I want to elbow him so hard, but I just smile and play along. Leo's teammates are giving him jealous looks—well, all except Anson. He's glaring at me.

"You're not even eating?" Suki asks, shocked.

She knows me well.

"I will be," Leo says, giving me a wicked grin. "As soon as we get in the house."

My stomach does a full flip, the thought of him tearing off his suit jacket and tie making me warm all over. What if every inch of his chiseled, hard body was committed to my pleasure? And what if I could find out how he likes to be touched, and what makes him lose control?

I tug on his hand, the fantasy sex I'm playing out in my mind the most action I've had in a very long time.

"See you in the morning, boys," he says. Then he looks at me and says, "How lucky am I?"

So this is what it feels like. I've never understood how Suki fell so hard and fast for Carter. She let go of her fear and trusted him not to destroy her. And this is why. He looks at her the way Leo is looking at me right now. Like she's everything to him and no woman could ever measure up to her.

Leo's faking it, of course. So I don't know exactly what it feels like, but I can imagine. It makes me wish I hadn't been so thorough in convincing Leo I hate him.

We walk out to his car, where he opens the passenger-side door for me. "I thought I'd need to call an Uber, but I'll be okay to take you home."

I pinch my brows together, confused. "What's going on?"

He shakes his head and says, "Just get in."

I do, and then he closes my door and walks around to the driver's side. Once he's behind the wheel, he takes several long, deep breaths. I fight my curiosity and give him about half a minute of quiet before I speak.

"Did you get bad news?" I ask gently.

He starts the car. "No."

"Did one of your teammates say something shitty to you?"

131

"Nothing like that. I'll be fine tomorrow."

But he's not fine right now. I can't just go home knowing something is so wrong that he can't even get through dinner with his teammates.

"Is it something to do with a woman you're seeing?"

He sighs heavily. "Mara, stop interrogating me. I just need to go home, that's it."

"Is someone waiting for you there?"

"No."

He's getting aggravated, but the irony is, we were on opposite sides of this exact argument yesterday.

"Are you being melodramatic?" I ask.

That gets me an almost smile. He seems to think about something for a few seconds before he says, "It's something I have medication for at home. That's it. Not a big deal."

"So then why are we going to my apartment first? Let's go get your medication."

He shifts and clears his throat. "No, it's okay."

"Come on, Leo. Don't be like this. I can take an Uber from your house if I need to. If you're sick enough you couldn't even get through dinner, let's go get your medication."

"It's not like that. Don't worry about it, I'll be fine."

"This is bullshit. After the way you pushed me last night, and I spilled my guts to you? I'm not even asking what you have, I'm just saying go get your medication."

I can see the tension in his jawline as he says, "Fine."

Though I want to keep talking to him, I know if I say the wrong thing, he'll change his mind. So I sit and worry about all the things that could be going on with him. Whatever it is, it can't be easy to keep up with his schedule and the grueling physical requirements of hockey.

"Are you probably going to be alive in five years?" I ask, the not knowing killing me.

"Unless you kill me first, most likely."

"What, like deliberately? Or do you mean the burden of even speaking to me might do you in?"

He flicks a quick look at me. "Both."

"Yeah, you're for sure being melodramatic."

He laughs softly. "Maybe."

A few minutes later, he pulls into a neighborhood of condos in a golf course community. It's upscale, but nothing like Carter and Suki's house. He uses an opener to open the double garage of one, pulling inside.

There's not much in it. A bicycle. A bunch of golf stuff. A Cleveland Crush team poster hangs on one wall.

I get out of the car when he does, but he turns and stops me as I follow him.

"I can just go grab it real quick."

"Can I come see Birdie?"

His dog grew on me in the time we spent together at Carter's. She's one of those dogs you can tell is grateful just to be warm and fed, because she hasn't always been cared for.

He hesitates, then nods. I'm expecting his house to look like a dungeon or something, but it's just an average bachelor pad. Functional furniture, white walls and minimal decor.

Birdie is waiting for him, her tail swishing back and forth as soon as she sees him.

"Hey, girl," he says, bending down to pet her.

"Want me to take her out?" I ask, walking over to pick up her leash from the kitchen counter.

He practically lunges at me. "No, don't."

I set the leash back down and say, "Sorry."

Cringing, he shakes his head. "No, you didn't do anything wrong. It's ..." He sighs heavily and walks over to the kitchen sink, picking up a pill bottle from a row of bottles next to the sink. "I didn't want you to see these, that's all."

"Oh." I take a step toward the door, wishing I hadn't pushed him to let me come in. "I'll just meet you at the car."

He shakes his head, taking a pill from one of the bottles. "It's okay. The meds are for anxiety and depression. So there you go. You were right all those times you said I'm not right in the head."

I open my mouth to respond, but nothing comes out. Probably because I'm the world's biggest asshole and there's literally no response to what he just said.

CHAPTER FIFTEEN

Leo

"I DIDN'T MEAN—I'M so sorry, Leo. When I said that, I was just being brash and reactive. I never really thought that."

I shrug as I walk over to the fridge to get out a bottle of water. "It's the truth."

"No, it's not. I was being an asshole. Just like all the times I said you probably have to pay for sex—obviously, you don't. I just run my mouth. It's a problem."

After twisting off the cap of the bottle, I put the pill in my mouth and swallow it with water. Even though it doesn't work this quickly, I immediately feel better. This medication is for situational high anxiety, and I really need to start carrying it with me all the time.

"I don't care about the shit you've said about me," I

say. "Just please don't tell anyone about this. No one knows."

"It's not something to be ashamed of. I took depression medication in college, and I went to therapy. Both things really helped me."

I nod. "I go to therapy, too. But I'm nowhere near ready to go off my meds."

"So what? Who says you need to?"

Birdie is nudging at Mara's hand, trying to get some attention. Mara sits down on the kitchen floor, letting my dog into her lap.

"Did it come out of nowhere tonight, or was it something specific?"

Her tone is conversational, like we're discussing our schedules or the weather. I expected her to be taken aback when I told her, and I'm not sure how to handle her reaction.

"Uh ..." I sigh deeply. She already knows about my mental health issues and medications, so why not just tell her everything? "I have a knee injury, and I've been hiding it. When I got hit tonight, it made it worse. Now the pain is constant. So I'm fucked."

She smooths her hand over Birdie's back as she speaks. "Because you won't be able to play?"

"Yeah. Our team trainer knows I'm hurt. I don't know what the fuck I did to give it away, but she knows and she wants to look at it. It's a torn meniscus. I'll either need major rehab or surgery. I might never be the same again."

"You might be even better, though, once you're not trying to play with an injury."

I run a hand through my hair. She doesn't get it. Hockey is my life. I don't know who I am without my team and my routine.

"The fear of not making it back is real, though," she says. "I don't mean to minimize it."

I don't know if it's my medication kicking in or if it's because she didn't flip out when she found out about my conditions, but I'm feeling more relaxed. Comfortable, even.

"Are you hungry?" I turn on some lights. "I can make us something to eat."

"I'm starving." She gets up from the floor. "I'll help."

I scan the contents of my fridge. "We could have some omelets ready pretty fast."

"Yeah, I love a good omelet."

She rolls up the sleeves of her sweater and washes her hands at the sink. That's when I see part of my last name on the back of the sweater, her long dark hair obscuring some of the letters. I stop breathing for a few seconds.

"You did that," I say.

She looks over her shoulder at me, her brow furrowed. "Hmm?"

I shake my head, trying to clear my head. "The sweater with my name."

"Oh. I asked Suki to get me one."

She turns, drying her hands on a towel. "Want me to crack the eggs? I'm freakishly good at it."

"You wanted to wear it?"

She smiles, looking confused. "Are we still on the sweater? Yeah, I wanted to wear it."

I forget the ingredients on the island. "Can I tell you something?"

"Of course."

"I should've looked away. That day in the bathroom. I guess I was being a desperate pervert, because I think you're beautiful. I never meant a single thing I said about your ... bush. I've fantasized about it a thousand times, just as it was that day."

Her lips part. "You don't have to say that. I was in the shower to shave my bikini line, because we were getting in the hot tub, and I wanted you to ... it doesn't matter."

She looks away. My blood pounds with excitement as I walk around to the side of the kitchen island she's standing on, tipping her chin up so we're at eye level.

"It matters," I say softly. "What were you going to say?"

She wets her lips with the tip of her tongue, vulnerability in her expression. "I wanted you to look at me. And like me. I borrowed one of Suki's swimsuits that's too small for me because it makes my boobs look amazing."

Her words make my cock stiffen. "When have your boobs ever not looked amazing?"

A smile dances on her lips. "Fair point. But you know what I mean. This suit is like a custom-made

138

display case for my tits. I wanted you to want me. And when you saw me like that ... I lost my shit."

I cup her jawline, smoothing the pad of my thumb over her lower lip. Her eyes widen slightly. "There's never been a time since the first time I saw you when I didn't want you."

She pinches her brows together. "Not in that moment. With the green clay mask on my face and conditioner in my hair?"

"Are you kidding? I wanted to get in the shower with you. And then, once you started yelling at me every time you saw me, I wanted you even more. You're ... wild. Like the most exotic flower that only grows in places man can't get to. I could only admire you from afar, but never get close."

"Maybe ..." She swallows, looking nervous. "Maybe that's the appeal, that you couldn't have me. Maybe if you could, you'd be bored."

My grin almost turns into a laugh. "Mara, the one thing I'd never be around you is bored."

"I don't want to disappoint you."

I put my hands on her waist and lift her onto the kitchen island, keeping my hands on her. She cradles my face as I rest my forehead against hers. "You'll never disappoint me. I'm not the playboy you think I am. I haven't been with a woman in a long time, because if it's not special, I don't want it."

I grab the sweater and gently pull it up over her head, tossing it aside. Underneath, she's wearing a tight black camisole. My anxiety attack is a distant memory as I bend down and kiss her jawline, then her cheek. Her breath is warm on my face, coming in uneven little bursts.

When I kiss her, she slides her arms around my neck, moving closer to me. Her mouth is soft and warm. She tastes like cinnamon gum. When I put a hand on her lower back and press her closer to me, deepening the kiss, she moans softly.

I'm rock hard, and she knows it. She wraps her legs around my waist, pressing her core into my erection. We've only kissed, and this already feels more intimate than anything I've had with other women.

Mara is the only one who has seen all of me. She knows my secrets and wants me anyway. All those heated arguments were foreplay, and I want to devour her and savor her in equal measure.

She pulls off the camisole, revealing a lacy, pale-pink bra. I trail a fingertip over the silky fabric, her nipple pebbling beneath my touch.

"Are you sure?" I ask her.

"Yes. I have a birth control implant." She grabs my tie, just holding on to it and not moving. "Are you sure?"

"Completely."

She pulls on my tie, our mouths hungry when they meet. It's a tangle of lips and teeth and tongues as we work together to get my tie and dress shirt off. She slides off the island and takes her shoes and leggings off, leaving her in socks and underwear.

I get the rest of my clothes off in record time,

taking satisfaction in the widening of her eyes when she sees my cock.

"I would've been so much nicer if I'd known you're that big," she says, a smile playing on her lips.

"Bullshit." I grin back at her, lifting her back onto the island.

I peel her socks off one at a time and drop them to the floor. Her underwear goes next. She's leaning back on her elbows, shivering slightly as my gaze roves over her.

"My fantasy come true," I murmur. "You're so beautiful."

I bend, planning to bury my face between her legs, but a sharp pain in my knee makes me cringe and stop.

"Fuck. Sorry. It's my knee."

"Don't worry about it."

She's off the island in an instant, taking my hand. "Take me to your bedroom."

My condo is all on one level, so I lead her down the hallway to my bedroom, closing the door so Birdie can't follow.

"Lie down."

It's a silken, seductive command. And even though I want to obey, I hate that she had to take over because of my injury.

"I can still fuck you," I say. "You lie down."

The room is dark, but there's enough moonlight coming in around the blinds that I can see her unfastening her bra.

"Leo, lie down," she says again. "Please."

I shove the covers from my unmade bed and lie on my back, my cock throbbing with need as she gets on the bed and straddles me. She doesn't wait for me—she lines the head of my cock up to her slick pussy and moves, moaning with pleasure when I'm not even halfway inside her.

I trail my fingertips down her stomach, sliding my thumb over her clit. She rocks her hips and takes more of me, my groan drowning out her moan.

"Do you like it?" she whispers.

"I fucking love it. Your body is the most incredible thing I've ever felt."

I can't tell if her cry as I sink deeper inside her is pleasure or pain. I hold on to her hips, supporting her but letting her set the pace.

"Fuck." She moans as she starts riding me, her outline just visible in the room's dim light.

I could come so fast, but I make myself hold on. Every one of my senses is steeped in hot, clawing desire for her. When she cries out my name, it's all I can do not to grip her hips and drive myself into her as hard as I can.

This is what it feels like to be two halves of a whole. The soul-deep craving and satisfaction coursing through me isn't something I could ever feel alone. I didn't plan to let Mara past my walls, but I'm so fucking glad it happened.

"Oh my god." She's breathless, riding me hard and fast.

"Let me see it all," I say, pressing my fingers into her

hips harder. "Show me what you look like when you get that sweet pussy off on my cock, baby."

"Oh, fuck, Leo." She grinds into me even harder.

"Yeah, let go for me." I grind the words out, barely holding on to the shred of control I have left.

She cries out again, so loud and primal I know she's coming hard. I follow, groaning powerfully as I hold on to her hips and let myself go.

Still catching her breath, she moves off me and lies down on her back. "What just happened?"

There's satisfaction and amusement in her tone. Fortunately, I don't hear any regret.

"I think we stopped hating each other," I say lightly.

She laughs. "I can't promise I'll never get mad at you again, though."

"Understood."

She rolls onto her side, so I move onto my side, too.

"I don't want things to be awkward with us," she says.

"They won't."

"I know you have to be up early, so I'll get dressed. We don't have to cuddle. Can you still give me a ride home?"

"I'll take you home, but not yet."

She yawns. "Why not yet? Do you want an all-night fuckathon? Because I'm not sure I can do it."

"I don't want you to go. I'll make the omelets and we can eat in bed and get some sleep. I'll take you home on my way to the airport."

There's a moment of quiet before she says, "Okay. Make mine extra cheesy."

I kiss her once, then again. I've never felt so content this soon after a panic attack, even with medication. I don't know if it was the sex or just Mara being here.

It feels damn good, though. I'm not spiraling over my knee anymore. I want to just be here with her tonight—both physically and in my head.

CHAPTER SIXTEEN

Mara

I SET down a heavy case of files on my assistant Missy's desk, every muscle in my legs hurting.

"Do you have any ibuprofen?" I ask her.

"Of course. I'm the office dealer, remember?" She opens her desk drawer and takes out a large pill organizer. "I'll help you carry those to the courtroom."

"No, it's okay." I take the two pills she offers. "Thanks."

"Are you sure you're okay? You look like you're not feeling well."

It's probably the dark circles beneath my eyes making her think that. I got maybe two hours of sleep last night at Leo's. But other than the exhaustion, I'm amazing.

We tried to get some sleep after eating our omelets

in bed, but our hands and lips were roaming, and a second, slower session of sex was inevitable. That's why everything from my waist down hurts. Leo bent me and moved me into positions that used muscles I'm not sure my body even knew it had.

It's always been hard for me to come a second time in one night, but he was patient, reading my body like a song he knows by heart. He took his time getting me there, and I saw stars. Sex with any other man is ruined for me.

"Just tired," I tell Missy.

She arches a brow. "Good tired?"

Missy and I share personal stuff when we're alone. She's recently divorced and has also been in a long-term sex drought.

"Amazing tired." I smile, knowing I have heart eyes.

"Yeah, girl. Good for you."

I take the pills, swallowing them without water because I need to get to court. Jayden is off today, so I'm flying solo.

It's been nearly impossible to keep my mind on work today. What happened with me and Leo last night came out of nowhere. I knew we were slowly becoming friends, but I had no idea he'd ever thought about more than that with me.

There's never been a time, since the first time I saw you, when I didn't want you.

I keep replaying his words in my head, and I never stop feeling giddy when I do. I thought being a strong, independent woman meant I didn't care about a man feeling smitten with me. Especially Leo Abbott.

Everything changed when he opened up to me about his anxiety and depression, and his knee injury. He trusted me with his most closely guarded secrets, and I want to show him he was right to trust me.

For more than a year now, I've seized every opportunity to make fun of him. I'm not proud of how I've acted. I could see all over his face last night that he wasn't sure if he'd get a sharp comment about his mental health medication.

Even a tall, strong man like him, who seems to have it all, has vulnerabilities. When we tried to sleep, neither of us could. I whispered to him several times, asking if he was awake and he said he was because he couldn't believe I was really there with him.

It was the same for me. When he was spooned around my back, his arm tucking me close to him, I'd close my eyes to sleep and I couldn't stop smiling. Because he wanted me to stay. Because we'd just had the most incredible sex ever. Because he was so warm and solid against me.

I did finally drift off around three thirty a.m., but we had to be up at five thirty so he could get me home and make his flight on time. We both stole looks at each other the whole drive, and he walked me to my door and kissed me goodbye.

I've felt like I was floating since I walked into my apartment. I'm not a woman who falls head over feet for any man, but I'm feeling like I could right now.

It's probably good that he just left for a six-day road trip. Maybe the time away from each other will help me return to my usual, more cynical self.

The space outside the courtroom I'm walking to is filled with traffic defendants. People of all ages are waiting for their hearings, and I'm the prosecuting attorney for all of them.

"Hey, you work here?" a man asks me. "I can't find my attorney."

"I'm sorry, I can't help. Try the bailiff."

Once I get into the courtroom, I tie my long hair back, already sweating, and regret my decision not to slam an energy drink earlier. My eyelids are heavy. I could easily curl up on the table I'm sitting at and sleep for the next eight hours.

But duty calls. And last night was so worth today's exhaustion.

IT'S SOMEWHERE between three and four p.m. when I walk back into the office after making a run to the coffee shop a block away from the courthouse. I powered through my hearings and all the work I needed to finish today. My late lunch consisted of a chocolate chip cookie and a cold brew coffee, and between the caffeine and the sugar, I know I'll make it through the workday without falling asleep face down on my desk.

"Look what just arrived," Missy says, gesturing at a

vase bursting with red-stemmed roses. There must be at least two dozen, and they smell heavenly.

"Those are gorgeous. Who sent them?"

She lowers her brows. "I guess you'll find out when you open the card."

I pull my drink away from my mouth. "They're for *me*?"

She grins. "The card says Queen of Mean Mara Torres."

I laugh, imagining Leo placing an order and asking for the card to be signed that way. How did he pull this off? He's in Tampa right now.

I snatch the card, my stomach somersaulting with excitement. Red roses sent to my office. That's a first for me.

When I pull the card out of the envelope, the words on it make me giddy.

Thanks for an amazing night. I can't wait to see you again.

Leo

The message on the card means more to me than the roses. I carefully tuck it back into the envelope. This is the first time since last night that I've felt scared.

I'm already in over my head with Leo. We were both there for each other in moments of vulnerability, and it brought us closer. But this isn't a real relationship. When whatever it is runs its course, it's going to hurt. I don't know how I'll be able to be around him at fondue nights or all the other times I see him—because of Carter—and not be visibly upset.

"You don't look happy," Missy says.

I sigh softly. "I am. Just running through all the ways this could go bad."

"Girl." She gives me a stern look. "Don't do that."

She's about to give me a full-blown lecture when she's interrupted by Gayle walking into our little section of the office.

"Mara, can we talk in your office?" she asks.

"Sure."

I'm immediately tense because I can tell my boss is unhappy about something. Was it one of the cases from this afternoon? Did I do something I shouldn't have?

As soon as we're alone inside the office Jayden and I share, I close the door.

"This office is terrible." Gayle shakes her head as she looks around.

She's right. It's dark and depressing and even though it's been years since it was repurposed from a janitorial supply room into an office, it still smells like Pine-Sol.

"We're not here all that much," I say.

"Have a seat."

My stomach churns nervously as I sit down behind my desk, Gayle taking Jayden's chair. We have the fronts of our desks pushed together so we can share the space for our many files and pass them back and forth easily. When we need to meet with people, we use a conference room. No one but us usually sees this office.

"Our IT people reached out to me about an email that came in for you this afternoon," Gayle says. "You know there are certain words that get flagged by the system."

My eyes widen and I swear my heart stops. Surely none of my friends would send a profane message to me here, even as a joke. If all my hard work to make a respectable name for myself here has been compromised by someone's hairy balls meme, I'm going to lose it.

"I'm so sorry," I say, feeling sick. "I don't—"

She cuts me off. "It's nothing for you to apologize for. I just need to make you aware. The message gets removed from your inbox when it's flagged."

I stop short, confused. "I guess I'll need you to elaborate."

The corners of her mouth turn down slightly in a frown. "The message said, 'You're dead, bitch.' We unfortunately get messages like that in this line of work."

I pinch my brows together, shocked. "And you're sure it was intended for me?"

She nods. "The sender thought he was being clever and masking his IP address, but the sheriff's department has already traced it to a one-block radius of Drake Harn's address."

My jaw drops. "Drake Harn? Libby's husband?"

"Yes, Bruce filled me in on the conversation you had

with her, and you did nothing wrong. Domestics are the hardest cases we work on. Just be vigilant, because the sheriff's department has been unable to locate Drake. Don't walk to your car alone, keep your doors locked, and report anything suspicious. The sheriff's department will be patrolling your apartment building."

I sit back in my chair, still in disbelief. "Patrolling my building? You mean driving past it once every hour?"

"Pretty much. It's all they're willing to do at this point."

I rub the bridge of my nose, knowing there's no way I'll be able to sleep at my apartment tonight, even though I'm exhausted.

"You're welcome to my guest room if you want it," Gayle says.

The thought of my boss seeing me in my pajamas— or me seeing her in hers—is so awkward I almost cringe.

"Thanks. I'll stay with a friend for now."

She stands. "I know it's alarming, but we all get these messages. Drake won't be able to hide for long, and he'll be arrested as soon as he pops up."

I guess that's something. "Maybe he'll get jail time and Libby can have her baby without him around."

Gayle sighs heavily. "She's pregnant?"

"Yeah. Bruce was right; there was no way I was going to be able to convince her to testify when he couldn't. But I had to try."

"You were right to try. I don't want anyone in my office who thinks of victims as case numbers. These are people. Abuse is a hard cycle to break."

I rest my elbow on my desk and my chin on my hand. "I've been thinking about Libby. She works at a gas station. She has no family around here to help her."

"We give victims contacts for local organizations that can help. There's always a way out."

"Yeah, you're right."

"Joe Burris is the deputy working on this case. Call him if anything comes up, okay?"

"I will."

"I'll tell the bailiffs you need an escort to your car until this is resolved."

"Okay."

She leaves my office and I just sit there in silence for a few minutes, my concern growing. My light, happy mood is gone now.

I wish Leo was home. I'd call him and ask him to pick me up and bring me to his house. Even though I know this happens to assistant state attorneys regularly, it's different when it's happening to me. I saw the photos of the injuries Drake gave Libby. He's already in trouble, so he has nothing to lose.

But Leo isn't an option, and I don't want to risk putting Suki and the girls in danger, so I call Dex.

CHAPTER SEVENTEEN

Leo

BASH LOOKS from me to Melina, then back to me, his brow furrowed.

"Why is she staring at you?"

"No clue."

It's a lie, obviously, but now's not the time to tell Bash what's going on with my knee.

Melina was waiting for me on the airport runway this morning, and she was pissed. Since I slipped out of the locker room last night, she couldn't examine my knee before the road trip.

Every step I take hurts at this point, and I have to work hard to play it off like nothing hurts. She watches my every move, just waiting for me to slip up.

My team needed me tonight. We won 3–2, and I scored one of our goals. As I celebrated the goal with my teammates, I wondered if Mara was watching at home.

I can't stop thinking about her. The sex was off the charts, but it was the time we spent in bed after that's still swirling around in my head. We laughed and talked, not sleeping much, even when we tried.

She's sexy as hell when she's sharp and fierce, but when she's soft and exposed, she's even sexier. It was hard as hell to kiss her goodbye and leave this morning. And I'm on a six-day road trip, so it's going to be a long wait until I can see her again.

Carter comes over to the locker room bench Bash and I are sitting on, wearing just a T-shirt and underwear.

"Denton has to get his sac stitched," he says.

"Oh, fuck," I say. "From that stick to his groin?"

He nods. "Lucien's gonna fuck Tyler Hortman up when we play them next. Denton almost passed out when he saw how swollen his nuts are."

"Yeah, can't blame him."

Denton's a rookie, and he's a hell of a nice kid. He's nineteen, and he reminds me of myself at his age. There are two brothers in the league—Tyler Hortman and Tyson Hortman—and they play for different teams. Tyler's a brawny enforcer, and Tyson's a goalie.

I have to do a quick interview when I leave the locker room, and I don't hate it as much as I usually do. Probably because I know I won't be asked for an interview again anytime soon—once Melina makes me get an MRI of my knee.

I keep my phone turned off during games, and when I turn it back on, I find a text from my dad.

Dad: Great game. Saw your interview. Very proud.

Smiling at the screen, I text him to say thanks. He's actually a good conversationalist in person, but over text he uses as few words as possible. I was hoping for a text from Mara, but I don't see one.

I'm going back and forth on whether I should text her when I decide, fuck it. I quickly type out a message to her.

Leo: Hey, thought about you all day. Hope work was good.

"Abbott."

I look up and find Melina giving me a serious glare. She's a good trainer and I feel slightly bad for ducking out on her last night.

"Yeah, I'm coming."

When I get up from the bench, she turns and leads the way into the training room. I get on the table, waiting for her to ask if she can examine me.

"Torn meniscus," is all she says.

I shrug. "Might be."

"Should I bother telling you about how much worse you could injure yourself by continuing to play on it?"

I shake my head.

"You might not need surgery. We might be able to rehab it. But if you keep playing on it, you're definitely going to end up needing surgery."

I don't want surgery. But I also don't want to leave

my team midseason, even if it's just for several weeks of rehab.

"I can tell by the way you're walking what it is," Melina says. "I could examine it, but I don't need to. This is your body, man. You have to take care of it."

I sigh heavily. "It was only bothering me a little until recently."

"You need to stop playing and get an MRI as soon as we get home."

I want to say no. But something inside me shifted last night when I was with Mara. I always thought that if I projected strength, it didn't matter what was really happening to me on the inside.

When I told her about my anxiety and depression, and she didn't look at me any differently, I realized how wrong I've been. I've fought my weaknesses for so many years. Lied and said I was fine when I wasn't. I'm tired of that shit.

I nod, feeling anxious and relieved at the same time. It hurts like hell to play like this.

"I know it's hard, but you'll get through this," she says.

I feel numb as I walk back out to the locker room and call Carter and Bash over to a quiet corner.

"I'm pretty sure I have a torn meniscus in my left knee," I say.

Carter puts his hands on his head, his expression grim.

"Fuck," Bash says.

I hate disappointing them, but I'm not at one hundred percent, and I can't keep faking it forever.

"I'm sorry," I say.

Carter draws his brows together. "Don't be sorry. Shit happens. We'll get through it."

"Or not." I look away, my pulse pounding.

"What's that mean?" Bash asks. "You're not gonna die from a meniscus tear."

I shrug. "No, but I might not make it back if I get surgery."

"You'll make it back." Carter puts his hands on my shoulders. "I know you, man. Don't sweat this."

I almost laugh, wanting to tell him I sweat absolutely everything. Anxiety is a part-time job for me at times. But I'm not ready for anyone but Mara to know about it yet.

"I'm beat," I say. "I hardly got any sleep last night. I'm going back to the hotel to crash."

We usually take off for the next city after finishing a game, but our team plane is getting a part replaced, so we're flying out in the morning. It'll be an early morning, but at least I get to sleep in a bed tonight.

I go back to my locker and get my stuff, seeing a text back from Mara.

Mara: Work wasn't great. I'll talk to you about it when you get back. Great game tonight. Thank you for the roses, they're beautiful.

I frown at the phone. Like hell are we talking about it when I get back. We're talking about it tonight.

"YOU'RE AT DEX'S?"

I'm on the ride back to my hotel, and I'm about to jump out of my skin.

"It's probably nothing, but I'll sleep better here tonight."

Mara's drowsy voice reminds me of last night—or maybe I should say early this morning—when she was safely in my arms in bed.

"Why do you think it's nothing? Does Dex have a security system? Are the police out looking for this guy?"

"Slow down." There's a smile in her voice. "I'm okay, Leo. Dex has a security system and a dead bolt."

I want to board the next flight back to Cleveland. This guy who threatened her is dangerous and unhinged. It's making me sick that I'm so far away from her right now.

"If the police know who it is, why is he not in jail?"

"They're looking for him."

I about blow a gasket. "So he's on the loose?"

"The last I heard, he was, but they could have him in custody by now."

I run a hand through my hair, my blood pressure rising with every word she says. "Can you call and find out?"

"It doesn't work that way."

She sounds so calm and relaxed. Which is making me even more *uncalm* and *unrelaxed*. This maniac could be waiting around any corner for her. He could fuck with her car or break into her apartment.

"This is part of the job," she says. "People don't like getting fined or put in jail or having their loved ones put in jail. I'm taking precautions, I promise."

I sink into the back seat of the SUV I'm in, my heart still thudding like a drum.

"I'm not used to having someone to worry about," I say. "Am I moving too fast?"

She hums in amusement. "No. But isn't it funny that going balls deep is fine, but if you show you care, you're worried about moving too fast?"

"I want to do things the right way," I say, unsure how this conversation got so off course. "Not that I know what that is when we've already known each other for a year."

"You're doing things perfectly. I loved the roses so much."

I lower my voice, not wanting my driver to hear what I'm saying. "It's hard for me to not know whether you're safe. Even though we're ... new."

"I'm safe. Dex is taking me to work tomorrow and picking me up after, so we can go to trivia and then come back to his place. I won't be alone."

"Okay."

"Tell me something."

Her voice casts a spell over me. I was all worked up, and just the sound of her voice calms me. "What do you want to know?"

"Anything. I just want to hear your voice."

I should say something nice about her, but instead I say, "I talked to our trainer about my knee. I'm going on the injured reserve and getting an MRI when I get home."

"You did? Oh, Leo. I'm so glad you did. What made you change your mind?"

"You."

She laughs lightly. "I love it when I get credit for something I wasn't even trying to do. Seriously, this is really good news. So what happens from here?"

I sigh deeply. "The MRI will help the doctors see how bad the tear is. They'll either recommend rehab or surgery. Either way, I'll be out for at least four weeks."

"Wow. How are you feeling about that?"

"I don't even know. It hasn't even sunk in yet. It will tomorrow, when I'm not dressing for the game."

She yawns, and I remember our lack of sleep last night. "You don't regret last night, do you?"

"Not at all. It was incredible. Do you regret it?"

"No. I haven't told Suki yet. Or anyone else. She's going to be so smug and satisfied when she finds out."

I grin. "Oh yeah? Why?"

"She pretty much called it. She thought she saw an attraction between us."

"I don't think I was ever great at hiding it."

"But you've called me a witch in like fifty-seven different ways. And the endless comments about my bush ... No man could ever fuck me without a machete and a road map. My bush maintenance should be covered by the feds because it's wildfire prevention. My bush is actually a wormhole that—"

I stop her. "I know. I was an asshole. I regret every word of it."

She hums a single note of amusement. "It's okay. I like a good spar every now and then. I like to think I give as good as I get."

I remember last night and all of our verbal bouts that led up to it. "Always. If not better. One of the sexiest things about you is how smart you are."

My car pulls up to my hotel and I get out, taking my bag and waving to the driver.

"I'm falling asleep," Mara says. "I was thinking ... instead of playing games about how often we should text and see each other, what if we're just totally honest? I'll start. I'll be hurt if I don't hear from you at all tomorrow. A text is fine, just don't ignore me."

"You won't need to worry about that. Get some sleep. And let me know if anything happens with the nutjob who emailed you."

"I will. Good night."

"Night."

CHAPTER EIGHTEEN

Mara

"HOW MANY BONES are in the average human body?" Dex can't even keep a straight face as he repeats the trivia question the host just asked. "I mean ... I've had many bones in mine, but I like to think my body is above average."

I give him a quick air high five from the other side of the table.

"Lainey, you're up," Suki says, her pen poised above our answer sheet.

"Two hundred and six," Lainey says.

My heart races as I glance at the faces of my closest friends. I'm a sharer, and I can't hold it in any longer.

"Speaking of, um, bones ... Leo and I are a thing now."

Suki gasps and covers her mouth with her hands. Harry just gapes at me. Lainey smiles. And Dex laughs.

"I knew it, I knew it, I knew it!" Suki is stomping her feet and practically dancing in her chair.

"Okay, focus, people," Dex says. "What's the bone in the forearm that is on the thumb side?"

Lainey draws her brows together, looking thoughtful as she studies her own arm. "Radius. Tell us more, Mara."

I try to think of the words, which is usually my thing, but it's hard. I can feel everything that's happened between me and Leo, but it feels impossible to describe it.

"I didn't even realize it was happening," I say. "I knew things were changing between us, but ..."

"I genuinely thought you two couldn't stand each other," Harry says.

"That was real."

"I don't think so," Suki says.

I roll my eyes and laugh. "Well, you'd know better than me."

"I always saw fire between the two of you. Not just a spark, but like a full-on bonfire. Leo doesn't get upset over anyone or anything but you."

That's true. He's always been very vocal about not wanting to be around me. And I've been the same way. Looking back, part of me meant it and part of me didn't. It was mostly my embarrassment over him seeing me naked that made me so defensive.

"Is that a good thing, though?" I ask.

Dex scoffs. "I don't even have to ask if the sex was good. I'm super jealous. You two could probably fuck a headboard all the way through the wall."

A few seconds of silence pass, all of them giving me an expectant look.

"What?"

Dex widens his eyes, looking impatient. "Are you new here? We're waiting to hear about the sex."

My cheeks get warm. "I don't want to talk about it."

"That's okay," Lainey says.

The other three, who have known me a lot longer, are all giving me looks of either shock or confusion.

"You made us listen to a full recounting of the guy who got diarrhea in the middle of sex with you and tried to finish," Harry says. "I can't unknow that."

Lainey cringes. "Really?"

"I made him leave and take my ruined bedsheets with him."

Dex snaps his fingers at us. "The funny bone isn't a bone. What is it?"

"Isn't it a nerve?" Suki says.

Lainey, our science expert, nods. Suki records the answer on our score sheet. Then she gives me a concerned look.

"You don't have to give details, but it was good, right? The sex?"

I can't help breaking into a huge smile. "It was great."

She reaches for my hand and squeezes it, her eyes shining with happiness. "I'm so happy for both of you. Let me know when you're ready to get pregnant."

"What?" Dex laughs. "What do you have to do with her getting pregnant?"

Suki's beaming with excitement. "We're going to try to get pregnant at the same time so we can have kids who are the same age. Lainey, we'd love for you to be part of it, too."

Lainey freezes, looking like the proverbial deer in headlights.

"That's *insane*," Harry says. "Can I suggest you both only get pregnant if and when you and your partner are ready?"

Suki glares at him. "Well, of course we'll do that. I just want to time it together if we can."

"Does Leo know Suki is planning your future children?" Dex asks me.

I shake my head. "We aren't even in a relationship. We just decided to stop hating each other like five minutes ago."

"I don't mean right now or anything," Suki says, looking aggravated.

"Next question, ready guys?" the trivia host says into his microphone. "What is the smallest bone in the human body?"

"Probably one of the bones in your pinkie," Harry says. "Or your little toe. Do those bones all have different names?"

"It's the stapes," Lainey says softly, making sure no

one at nearby tables can hear her. "A little bone in the ear."

"I had a little bone in my ear once when I dated a guy who couldn't see anything without his glasses," Dex says. "One minute I was asleep and then, bam—dick in my ear."

Harry looks horrified. "How fucking small was it if it fit in your ear? I might need to start a GoFundMe for this guy to get a procedure done."

"It didn't fit. It just made things weird."

The food we ordered arrives, and my stomach rumbles so loudly I'm surprised no one comments on it. I got fried mushrooms and potato skins, and it'll be the first food I've eaten all day.

"Are you guys down for some bridespeople outfit shopping next month?" Lainey asks.

She asked all four of us to be attendants at her wedding, which is so Lainey. It seems like she's been part of our group forever.

"Absolutely," I say. "Also, wedding bonus: I already know which groomsman I'm hooking up with."

Dex sighs dramatically. "Guess I'm the only single one now."

"You could get a date if you wanted to," Suki says.

"What, on a dating app? Where I could meet a guy who's either broke, a felon, or cheating on someone?"

Harry howls with laughter from the other side of the table. "Wasn't that guy Elian all three?"

"Oh, yes. He wanted me to be his boyfriend and his free lawyer so I could help with all of those situations, too. I really don't mind my single life. I do whatever I want whenever I want." He gives me a pointed look. "Hope you're ready to give all that up."

"Leo and I are a brand new thing. I don't think either of us knows what we want yet."

Lainey frowns. "What if you don't want the same things?"

I've been thinking about that question myself. My relationships haven't lasted long in the past. Sometimes it's been my fault and sometimes not. What if Leo doesn't want us to be exclusive? I can't do that. It's hard for me to open up and trust someone, and when I do, I'm giving them the power to hurt me. I'll be hurt if Leo still wants to see other people.

"I don't know," I say. "I guess we'll have to see."

"Just enjoy it for now," Harry says. "No one has all the answers from the time they start seeing each other."

"Have you and Aden talked about the future?" Suki asks.

"A little bit. We like where we are right now. Both of us work a lot of hours and that won't change."

"Well, I like him a lot," I say. "I think you two are good together."

"Thanks. I like him a lot myself."

The trivia host is on a break, so we're able to eat and talk without listening for the next question. Suki wordlessly puts some of her cheese fries on my plate and I put one of my potato skins on hers.

"Can we revisit my idea for a *Pretty in Pink*-themed bridal party at the wedding?" Dex asks. "I don't care if

Bash wants to do it with the groomsmen; it could just be us. As long as Lainey's maid of honor doesn't mind."

"I actually told her about it when I talked to her a few days ago," Lainey says. "She thinks it's a great idea."

I cringe and fake sob. "Has she seen Andie's dress, though? It's tragic."

"That's the point," Dex says.

"The point is looking stupid? Are you planning to dress like Duckie?"

"I'm more of a Blane."

"I just watched the movie with the girls a few nights ago," Suki says. "There are other dresses in the movie. I don't think any of us have to wear Andie's dress."

"I'd be open to that," I say.

Pink isn't my best color, but I'll wear it if that's what everyone else wants. Bash and Lainey are getting married on a beach in Hawaii, and I can't wait for the trip.

I'm almost finished eating when I get a text from Leo.

Leo: Hey, beautiful. I know you're probably at trivia, but I wanted to make sure everything's okay.

I smile at the screen as I write back.

Mara: Hey, everything is good. I slept great in Dex's bougie guest room bed with thousand thread count sheets. How are you?

Leo: I'd be better if you were here. Watching the game and not playing in it is my idea of hell.

Mara: What's the score?

Leo: We're down 2-1.

BRENDA ROTHERT

Mara: Try to think less about the game and more about the blow job I'll be giving you when you get home from the road trip.

Leo: You have my attention...

Mara: It's going to be a long, slow one. I want to taste every inch of you.

Leo: I've been thinking the same thing about you. I want you to sit on my face and get yourself off. And I want to tie you to my headboard and tease you until you're begging me to let you come.

Mara: Five more nights?

Leo: Feels more like fifty.

"All right, let's get back to it," the trivia host says. "Our next category is Westerns. Western movies, that is."

"Fuck," Dex mutters.

Mara: I have to put my phone away, I'm not allowed to have it out during the game. Text later?

Leo: Sure. Let me know when you're back at Dex's.

Mara: I will.

"In the movie *Butch Cassidy and the Sundance Kid*, what does Harvey Logan challenge Butch Cassidy to?"

From the looks on their faces, I know none of my friends know the answer to this. I don't either.

"A duel?" Suki whispers. "That's all I can think of."

"Makes sense," Lainey says.

She writes it down.

"Hey, was that Leo you were texting?" Lainey asks.

"Yes."

"Did he say who's winning the game?"

172

"They're down, it's 1–0."

"Fucking Winnipeg," she says.

"I can't believe he's allowed to text you during a game," Dex says.

"He's not playing tonight. He's injured."

Suki gives me a concerned look. "What happened?"

"He doesn't know for sure yet. He has to get tests done when they get back. Something to do with his knee."

"That's terrible. For him and the team."

I don't tell her what Leo said—that he's almost certainly going to be out for a while. It would get back to Carter.

I feel protective of Leo already. Even though there are lots of questions I don't know the answers to, I know I'll never share his secrets with anyone. Whether we stay lovers or just end up as friends, I never want to be his enemy again.

CHAPTER NINETEEN

Leo

IT'S BEEN the worst week I've had in a long time. I'm still traveling with my team, but I'm not part of it.

I go to meetings and meals with my teammates, but I'm on the outside. They're the ones bleeding and fighting for the wins. I'm just a spectator.

Melina examined my knee a few days ago and confirmed it's a torn meniscus. We both knew already, but it still sucked to hear her say it. I'm wearing a knee brace and it's feeling a lot better just from not playing hockey. I don't know if that means anything or not, though.

"How's the knee?"

Our team owner, Hudson McClain, approaches me in the tunnel outside the Winnipeg visiting locker room. He comes with us on road trips occasionally, and

BRENDA ROTHERT

he never misses a home game. Some teams have shitty owners, but we're fortunate. Hudson is a big fan of the game, but he never tries to micromanage his staff and coaches.

"It's better than it was," I say.

Hudson is in his late forties. He made his fortune in real estate starting in his twenties. He played hockey in high school, so he actually knows the game.

"You're standing out here wondering if we would've won if you'd played tonight," he says.

He read my mind. I don't deny it.

"Don't do that, Leo. Injuries are physical and mental. Murray talked about that in one of his sessions, remember?"

I nod. "I do. I remember a lot from that one."

Hudson hired a mindset coach to work with us a couple years ago. He comes in from time to time and gives presentations to the team and coaching staff, and he also works with us one on one when we need it. I've never done any one-on-one sessions because I worried he'd be able to tell I have anxiety.

I've got more of a fuck-it mentality at this point. I work harder than any player on this team. That's not arrogance; it's a fact. I'm early to practices and I stay late. I work with a trainer year round to stay in peak physical shape. I treat every game like a championship is on the line.

All this time, it was my own feelings of inadequacy that drove all that. I felt expendable—like if I wasn't giving everything I could physically and mentally give,

I'd be replaced. I'm tired of feeling that way all the time.

"Rest and rehab," Hudson says. "You'll be better for it when you come back."

"Thanks. How's Maya?"

He smiles at the mention of his teenage daughter. "Still testing my sanity on a daily basis. She tried to leave the house earlier in a shirt that was the size of a dishrag. Not on my watch."

I smile. "Did you make her change?"

"Hell yes, I did. I don't give a fuck what the style is. She wants to wear baggy pants with holes in them and shirts that are three sizes too small."

"How old is she now?"

"Fourteen going on thirty. One of her friends got her septum pierced, so Maya keeps asking me if she can too. Over my rotting dead corpse."

I shake my head. "Carter's getting there with Olivia. Kind of makes me hope I have boys when the time comes."

"I can't even imagine. A kid who just wears a regular T-shirt and regular pants? My blood pressure would drop thirty points."

The locker room door opens and Carter steps out and looks in both directions, his gaze landing on me.

"You're supposed to go to the will-call window."

"Will call? You mean where people pick up their game tickets? I have no idea where that is."

"Figure it out, dumbass."

"Why am I going there?"

He shrugs. "No clue."

Hudson furrows his brow. "Do you want me to send someone else? That's a lot of walking with your knee."

"No, I'll be okay. I just can't imagine why I have to go to the will-call window. This better be good."

"Let me get someone to drive you on a cart."

That would be a hell of a lot easier. "You sure?"

"You don't even know where you're going. Come on, let's get you some help."

———

A FEW MINUTES LATER, I'm bracing myself in a vehicle that looks like a golf cart with no roof, a Winnipeg staffer flooring it down the concrete-floored tunnel.

"Messed up your knee?" He gestures at the knee brace.

"Yep."

"That's no damn good."

There's a thick metal support post ahead, but he's still driving at top speed, heading straight for it.

"You see that, right?" I ask.

He turns the steering wheel hard at the last second. "I know this place like the back of my hand. Been driving these tunnels for years."

He picks up a remote and pushes a button. "Time for a little elevator ride."

We ride the elevator up, and as soon as the doors slide open, he floors the gas pedal again. I'm going to be lucky if I get to will call with nothing more than my knee injured.

There are still a few people in the arena's lobby, but they wisely give the driver a wide berth. I give as many apologetic looks as I can.

"Will call's closed," the driver says. "You sure this is where you're supposed to go?"

"I'm s—"

I stop when I see a woman with long dark hair sitting on a bench. Her hair is curtaining off her face, but I know it's her. Mara. My pulse pounds as we get closer.

She looks up and sees me, breaking into a smile.

"She's here for you?" the driver asks, slowing down.

"Yeah."

He whistles. "Lucky man."

When he stops, I get out of the vehicle and walk over to Mara.

"Surprise," she says, her eyes questioning. "Hopefully a good one."

"Are you kidding? Nothing could beat this. I can't believe you're here."

I wrap my arms around her waist and she hugs me around my shoulders. Her soft body and light citrusy smell make me forget my bad mood from the loss.

"I know it's crazy," she says, pulling away to look into my eyes. "You'll be home tomorrow. And it's Friday night, so I couldn't leave until after work and I just got here. Also Canada. But here I am."

I cup her face and kiss her. The kiss lingers for a few seconds until a horn beeps.

"It's a family venue," the driver cracks. "You two want a ride back down to the tunnel?"

I consider. "No, thanks. We'll get a ride."

"You got it, Mr. Abbott." He touches the tip of his hat. "Have a nice night."

He takes off, quickly reaching breakneck speed.

"What the hell?" Mara stares after him. "He has to be going at least twenty miles an hour."

"Yeah, it was an interesting ride up here." I smile at her. "Worth it, though. You wanted my body bad enough to fly to another country for it. I'm touched."

There's a wicked gleam in her eyes. "Will I be touched, though? That's what I want to know."

I grab her around the waist and pull her against me. "Damn right you will. I've been thinking about touching you every minute since I left."

A little worry line appears between her brows. "I'm so here for it, but is there a restaurant at your hotel? So I could maybe grab a sandwich? I've only had a bag of airplane peanuts."

"We'll order room service."

Her face lights up. "Yes, please. Are there any fluffy white hotel robes? I've never stayed at a place nice enough to get a robe."

I put my arm around her waist. "We'll get you a robe. Later. Right now, I'd rather get you out of your clothes."

We start the walk to the arena's exit, and as I hold the door open for her, her eyes lock onto mine.

"Thanks for being happy I came," she says. "I thought you might think it was too much."

I give her a serious look. "It's been a hard week, and it means a lot to me that you're here. More than you know."

I call us an Uber, and she snuggles into my chest as we wait for it to arrive. I only have my suit jacket, and it's freezing, so she tucks her hands inside the jacket.

Not only have I been frustrated about not playing all week, but I've also been worried about her because of the guy who sent the email. The police still haven't found him. She's been staying with Dex, but I don't know how long she'll want to keep doing that.

The team's hotel for this trip is understated on the outside, but very nice inside. I checked in earlier. I already have my key card. Teammates occasionally have their wives or girlfriends stay with them after a game on a road trip, but I never have.

It feels fucking amazing, walking across the hotel lobby with Mara at my side. I'm not playing any games with her—I like her a lot, and I want her to know it. I sent flowers and have been keeping in touch every day with calls and texts.

This is her version of not playing games—she wanted to come here, so she did. I'm going to be making sure she's happy about that decision.

As soon as the door to my room is closed behind us,

a switch is flipped inside me. I feel like a lion stalking its prey; I'm hungry for her, and I'm not feeling patient.

I take off my suit jacket and set it on a chair, then kick off my shoes.

"I missed you so fucking much," I say, already rock hard.

"I missed you, too. But I haven't even touched my vibrator. I only wanted you."

I pull off my tie and drop it on the floor. "Good girl. Take off your shirt so I can see your tits."

She slides out of her jacket and toes off her shoes, then strips off her shirt. Her bra is black, a little bow resting between her breasts.

I manage to get my dress shirt off before I pull her body against mine and kiss her. She moans and unfastens my pants, as eager as I am. I make quick work of releasing the brace from around my knee and tossing it aside.

Then we're all lips and tongues and roaming hands, both of us pulling each other's clothes off. Once she's completely naked and I'm only in boxers, I stand back and look at her.

"So beautiful," I murmur. "Lie down."

She gets on the bed, unfazed by the lights being on. Her confidence is a huge turn-on.

I take my time, kissing her ankles, her calves and her thighs. She gasps and holds onto my hair, trying to guide my head between her legs. I just laugh against her bare skin and kiss my way from her lower stomach to her breasts, teasing one nipple and then the other before I repeat the process.

"Please, Leo," she begs.

I fucking love the sound of my name on her lips. I reward her by licking her seam from bottom to top, making her whimper. As soon as my tongue touches her clit, she tugs on my hair hard and bucks her hips.

She's already close. I put a finger inside her, sucking her clit into my mouth. Within half a minute, she's coming, pulling on my hair and crying out my name.

Her eyes are glazed when she lifts her head to meet my gaze.

"Inside me," she says breathlessly. "Fuck me the way you like it until you come."

I tug off my boxers and bury my cock deep inside her. It's everything I've been fantasizing about and more. She puts her hands on my ass and pulls my hips closer, urging me on.

I want to fuck her in every imaginable position for the next hour, but that'll have to be our second round. My climax is approaching like an out-of-control freight train.

It hits me hard, the orgasm barreling through my entire body. I immediately feel a sense of fullness, like everything is what it's supposed to be in this moment.

"Your knee seems better," Mara says lightly.

"Maybe this is the right rehab for it. I could ask the team to put us up here for the next few weeks."

She laughs. "Let me know how that goes."

I kiss her jawline, her nose and her lips. "Ready for that room service?"

"You read my mind."

CHAPTER TWENTY

Mara

"Okay, people, last call for files," Missy says. "I'm going to file the old and pull the new *one time* today, and one time only. Speak now or forever hold your peace."

I can't help it, I laugh. Missy and Jayden both give me confused looks.

"Sorry, I'm just—" I laugh again, then clear my throat. "It's not appropriate workplace humor. I was just thinking if you spelled it p-i-e-c-e, that phrase would take on a whole new meaning."

Jayden exchanges a look with Missy. I think I know them well enough that they won't tell me to stop with the inappropriate jokes, but I'm not positive. I'm still a little punch drunk from my weekend with Leo.

"That's about a six out of ten," Jayden says. "It's not

bad, but usually you're sharper. Are you extra tired today?"

"No."

Yes. Leo helped me pack some things Saturday evening after I got home and I stayed with him the past two nights. We do sleep, just not a lot. I thought we'd spend the entire weekend in bed, and we did get in a lot of sex, but we also did things that surprised me.

We watched movies on his couch, Birdie switching back and forth between his lap and mine. We made breakfast together on Sunday, and then we went Christmas shopping together.

I usually don't wait so long to do my holiday shopping, but I've been busy with work and kept putting it off. Leo and I had the best time picking out gifts for our parents, our friends, and Carter and Suki's girls. He was patient, carrying bags and pretending to be interested in cosmetics.

"Missy, I'll do the the files," I say, standing up.

She laughs lightly, shaking her head. "Whoever this guy is, he gets my vote. You'd scrub the floors with a smile right now, wouldn't you?"

Probably not, because I'm sore from last night's sexcapades, but I ignore her question.

"This has nothing to do with Leo, I'm just trying to help."

"Ooh, Leo." She waggles her brows. "I don't think you've ever told us the name of anyone you were dating."

"Is that short for Leonard?" Jayden asks. "Did you pick him up at an old folks' home?"

I roll my eyes. "No, it's just Leo. That's his full name." I walk over to the file cart. "That's the list of files to pull?"

"Are you sure you want to do this?"

"Absolutely. You're swamped and I'm caught up."

She still doesn't look convinced, so I just take the cart. It's midafternoon, and I could use a break from the walls of my office to wake me up a bit.

"I'll make a drink run, too," I say. "Just us three, not the whole office. Text me your orders."

"Okay." Missy puts her palms up, not arguing. "Thanks, Mara. I appreciate you."

"No problem."

We have both digital and hard copy files because we need original signatures on paperwork. Once a case has a disposition, we return the hard copy file for storage. It involves an elevator ride down to the courthouse basement and a lot of walking.

When I reach the file storage area, the head file clerk, Andy, greets me with a smile.

"Hey, where's the boss?"

"I needed a break from the office, so I offered to come."

"We'll help you file," he says. "It's a slow day."

"Nice. Thanks."

The people who work in file storage every day are all about ten times faster than I am at filing. Within twenty minutes, there's only one file left on the cart.

"This one goes to the annex," Andy says.

"I can run it over."

"You sure?"

"Yeah, I'm going on a coffee run anyway."

"Thanks. If you give me your list, we'll pull new files and have them ready to go for you."

"You guys are the best."

Andy gives me a puzzled look. "Did you just win a big case or something? You look too happy for a regular Monday afternoon."

I can't stop smiling over my weekend with Leo, and I know I must look like a weirdo. Usually, I'm a scowling cynic, even though I tone down my moods a lot at work. But today, I feel like the main character in a rom-com, an upbeat soundtrack accompanying me.

"I'm just in a great mood," I say. "I'll be back soon."

I tuck the single file beneath my arm and head for my car. This evening will be the first time Leo and I get together with our friends since we became a thing. We're prepared for endless teasing. I'm actually looking forward to it. Suki and Lainey have both found their someones, and I wasn't sure I ever would. It's a stroke of luck that Leo and I already have the same close friend group.

My car is parked in a nearby deck, and I hurry there because it's so cold outside. I unlock my car and get inside, setting the file on my passenger seat. Even inside my car, it's still freezing.

"Don't move."

The voice coming from my back seat makes my

heart stop as I look in my rearview mirror. Shit. It was stupid of me to leave the courthouse without a bailiff. A rear side window of my car is broken out, and a man with wild blond hair and a lean, bearded face is in the car with me.

"Bitch, I mean it. You move and I'll pull the trigger."

Adrenaline floods my system so hard and fast I'm lightheaded. Drake Harn caught up with me.

"I won't move," I promise.

"I've got a gun up against your seat. If you want to live, do exactly what I tell you."

It's all I can do to keep breathing. I could get out of the car and run, but he could shoot me in the back. There's no one else around and nothing to hide behind but cars.

"Start the car and drive," he orders.

My hands shake as I get my key into the ignition. Statistically, if he takes me somewhere, I'm more likely not to survive. Thoughts of what he might do to me are racing through my head.

I don't see what choice I have. If I refuse to drive, he could shoot me and flee. Maybe I'll be able to get someone's attention while I'm driving and signal for help.

I keep my breathing steady as I drive, feeling on the verge of passing out. I was worried Drake might slash my tires or something; I genuinely didn't think this could happen.

"Libby and I were fine," he says, his voice harsh. "You fucked it all up. She wants to leave me."

What can I say to that? I did try to convince Libby

to testify against her husband and get out of her abusive situation. I look in every direction as I leave the parking deck. The only people I see walking have their heads down, trying to protect their faces from the icy wind.

"Get her to change her mind, or you're dead."

I glance in the rearview and see that Drake looks shaky, like he's on something. That makes a very bad situation even worse.

"You'll do it, right?" he asks, looking from side to side like he's worried someone will see us.

"Yes, I'll do it."

One of my classes in law school was about conflict de-escalation. I remember learning that keeping someone like Drake as calm as possible is best. Until I can find a way out of this, I need to do what he tells me.

My coworkers will wonder where I am when I don't come back. Hopefully they'll call the police. I'm not someone who ever slips out of work early without saying anything.

It takes about twenty-five minutes for me to reach the house on the outskirts of Cleveland that Drake directs me to. It has a bright-blue front door with a holiday wreath hanging on it.

He has a garage door opener, and he opens the double-stall garage with it. There's a small white sedan parked on one side of the garage.

"Park in there and don't move," he orders.

My heart is hammering with worry as I slowly ease my car into the garage. Being trapped with Drake, whether it's in his garage or his house, is a bad situation for me.

I think of Leo, wishing I could be back at his house, lying in his arms as we watch a movie together. It took me a long time to find my person; I'm afraid my happiness with him might be cut very short.

Drake opens the driver's side door, sneering down at me.

"She can't leave me," he says. "It's my baby, too."

I get my first look at his handgun, and I swallow hard against the bile rising in my throat.

"You're right," I say. "Tell me how I can help."

"Fuck you, bitch." He runs a hand through his hair, his eyes wild. "Get the fuck out of the car."

I'm close to pissing my pants. The situation gets really real as I step out of the car and he orders me to walk into the house. He has the end of his gun pressed up to my back.

I silently blink and let the tears in my eyes drop onto my cheeks so I can see clearly. When I open the steel door and walk into the house, I'm in the kitchen. Boxes of food, dirty dishes and empty beer cans line the counters. It smells like garbage. All the blinds are closed.

"Walk." Drake sticks the gun's muzzle in my back and I walk.

When I get around a corner, I stop breathing. In the middle of what I think is a living room, Libby is tied to a wood chair, her head slumped to the side. I'm not even sure she's alive until she picks up her head, her mouth dropping open in horror when she sees me.

"Oh my god." She gapes at her husband. "What did you do, Drake?"

"It's okay," I assure her. "Everything is okay."

"Tell her!" Drake yells from behind me. "Tell her she can't leave."

I purse my lips for a second, hating what I have to say to get through this. I just hope help is on the way.

"I was wrong, Libby." I clear my throat, fighting the wobble in my voice. "You should stay with Drake."

CHAPTER TWENTY-ONE

Leo

"I CAN'T JUST SIT HERE." I get up from a couch in Carter's living room and pace to the other side of the room. "There has to be something we can do."

"All we can do is wait," Suki says for the third time in the past twenty minutes.

It's been two hours since Suki called to tell me Mara's boss reached out to her, as Mara's emergency contact, to tell her Mara is missing.

Not officially, but the cops know something's wrong because of the threat from Drake and the fact that no one's been able to reach her since she left to take a work file somewhere.

Why the fuck would her boss let her leave the courthouse by herself like that? She's supposed to be getting escorted from her car and back to it again every day. If I had known she'd be alone in a parking deck, I would've been there.

"Do you think you can eat something?" Bash asks me.

"No, I can't fucking eat!" I roar, my worry and anger boiling over. "Sorry. I just—"

"Don't apologize, brother." Bash comes over and puts a hand on my shoulder. "You can punch me in the face if it'll make you feel better."

Dex took Olivia, Charlotte and Hattie out for dinner at Harry's restaurant because Carter and Suki wanted to shield them from what's going on with Mara. Carter, Suki, Bash and Lainey are waiting with me, and I know it's hard for all of us.

"I should be out there looking for her," I say.

"Looking where, though?" Carter says. "We don't know where she is."

My chest gets tight as I imagine what could be happening to Mara right now. My Mara. Our relationship developed unconventionally, but I'm all in. I've never been happier. Instead of feeling like a broken man hiding from himself, I feel like a whole man.

I don't know how to handle her being in danger. My chest pain worsens and I sit down, pressing a palm to my chest and taking a few deep breaths.

"You okay?" Lainey asks.

"I don't ... I can't ..." I breathe harder, struggling to find breath.

Carter kneels in front of me. "Slow down your

breathing, Leo. Take a nice deep breath through your nose and out through your mouth."

I try, but when I imagine some crazed maniac putting his hands on Mara, the pain intensifies and I double over.

"Whoa," Carter says. "Let's get him lying down."

Carter and Bash each take a side, awkwardly trying to get me to lie down. I'm so big that it's a struggle.

"My meds," I manage. "I need my meds."

"Where are they?" Lainey asks.

"In my car." I groan, the pain intensifying. Maybe this really is a heart attack. "The console. Atarax."

"Get his car keys," Suki says.

Bash digs them from my pocket, my vision starting to blur. I fight to get a breath into my lungs.

"Leo, listen to me," Carter says. "Slow. Slow your breathing."

"We need to call for an ambulance," Bash says.

"No," I manage, panting out a breath. "Anxiety."

Carter takes my hand and puts it on his chest. "Feel my breathing and follow it. In through your nose ... good. Now out. Slowly."

My chest still burns, but I feel the rise and fall of his chest, not thinking of anything but following it. I can't get sent to the hospital right now. Not when Mara needs me to be strong.

"Here it is," Lainey says from nearby. "And water."

"I'm putting a pill in your mouth," Bash says.

I open my lips and he drops it in.

"Take some water," he says.

Water spills from the bottle onto the couch as he tries to get it into my mouth. I move my head to make it easier and swallow the pill.

"Keep breathing," Carter says.

Once my breathing is under control, the pain lessens. I take a minute to get myself together before I sit up.

All four of my friends are giving me concerned looks. Bash and Lainey are standing together, his arm around her, and Carter and Suki are standing with Darling between them. Even the pig looks worried.

"I'm okay," I say, embarrassment setting in. "I have anxiety and depression and I take medication for both. That medication I just took helps me with anxiety attacks."

Carter furrows his brow. "How long has this been going on?"

I exhale deeply, scrubbing a hand down my face. "The anxiety and depression, around ten years. The medication, in the past year."

"Oh, Leo." Suki comes over and sits down next to me, putting a hand on my back. "I'm so glad you got help."

I can't even look at any of them. I feel like I just changed the way they'll see me forever.

"You didn't want us to know," Carter says.

I scoff. "Yeah, it fucking sucks. I had an anxiety attack after a game last year and Caroline spotted it. She made me start seeing a psychiatrist."

"Does it help?"

"Yeah. The meds and therapy help, but they don't just take it away."

"Everyone goes through shit like that," Carter says. "Anyone who says they don't is lying. I'm here anytime you want to talk."

"Yeah, me too," Bash says. "That was scary as shit, man. I hate that you thought you needed to go through that alone."

"I didn't want you guys to see me differently."

"That'll never happen," Carter says. "We've been through too much together."

I nod, my worries for Mara returning full force. "Mara knows, and she still—" I can't speak past the lump in my throat. "I need her to be okay."

Now I'm crying, for fuck's sake. The only embarrassing thing left to do in front of my friends is to shit my pants—that's probably next.

Suki leans against my shoulder. "I know. She's—" She jumps away from me, scrambling to pull her cell phone from her pocket. "Hello? This is she ... okay."

We all stare at her in complete silence. Her eyes are wide with fear. If Mara's not okay, I'm going to find the guy who hurt her and make him pay. I don't care about the consequences.

She was just doing her job. She was trying to help a woman escape her abuser. That guy needs to try taking a swing at me so he can find out what it's like to be outmatched.

"Okay," Suki says. "Thanks for the update. Call me as soon as you know anything."

She ends the call.

"They know where she is. She's at the home of the guy who sent her the email."

"Fuck." I stand up, putting my hands on my head. "Why haven't they gone in to get her? Where is it?"

"They aren't telling us where it is. Her boss told me the police are trying to get cameras and listening devices in. They think she's being held hostage."

A wave of nausea washes through me and I brace myself with a hand on the wall.

"And we're supposed to just wait?" I shake my head. "Why don't they just go in and fucking get her?"

"They have to be smart about it," Carter says. "You don't want them blasting their way in when she's in there."

I push off the wall, feeling like a caged beast. "I want to sprint out this fucking energy, but I can't because of my knee."

"Yeah, you're not doing that," Carter agrees. "Let's go cook dinner, just to give you something to focus on."

Suki was just starting to make lasagna when she got the call about Mara. We all return to the kitchen, Suki browning the meat while I chop onions and tomatoes.

"So what happened with Mara?" Lainey asks. "This guy is someone she encountered at work?"

I recount Mara's work on domestic violence cases and her talk with Libby.

"Wow," Suki says. "She hasn't told me any of that."

"And the woman's pregnant."

"Shit," Bash says. "I didn't know Mara dealt with stuff like that at work."

I finish chopping and Suki gives me a big block of mozzarella to shred, showing me how to use her automated shredder.

"Why don't we all have a glass of Mara's favorite wine?" Carter suggests. "I think she'd want us to."

Suki laughs, her smile sad. "She would, as long as we still had more."

Carter gets out a bottle of the red wine, pouring all of us a glass. I'm glad no one tries to do a toast, because now is not the time. I manage to drink almost half of my glass, following Suki's lead on layering the lasagna ingredients.

"I love her so much," she says softly. "I have all brothers, and she's been the sister I never had since we met." She meets my gaze. "I've never seen her happier than she's been since you guys got together."

"I've never been happier, either. She's—"

Suki drops a noodle and grabs a towel, quickly wiping her hands before taking her phone from her pocket.

"Hello?" She nods. "Yes." She listens for a few seconds and her shoulders sink. "She's okay?"

The entire room exhales with relief. The tightness in my body releases, and I feel like Jell-O.

"Okay, yes. Thank you so much."

Tears shine in her eyes when Suki ends the call and looks at me. "She's okay. The guy was holding her and his wife hostage, and his wife talked him into turning himself in."

"Thank God," Carter says.

Suki hugs me. I finally feel like I can breathe again.

"Now that we know she's okay, I need to go let Rosie out," Lainey says.

"I'll come too," Bash says. "We're gonna just take off and get some carryout, so you guys can have time with Mara. Tell her we're here if she needs anything."

"We will, thanks," Suki says.

Rosie is the puppy Bash brought home from the bachelor party. Lainey named her after a famous scientist. Bash bitched about the dog at first, but now his phone is full of puppy pictures he shows to anyone who will pay attention to him.

Once Bash and Lainey are gone, I leave Carter and Suki to finish dinner, sitting by myself in the living room. It's a relief to know Mara is safe, but I won't be able to fully relax until I can hear her voice or see her for myself.

There are so many things I want to say to her. I hold my phone in my hand, just staring at the screen. I know she'll call me as soon as she can. She's probably being questioned by the police.

The smell of baking lasagna makes me walk into the kitchen. Suddenly, I'm hungry, but I don't want to eat until I see Mara.

Darling comes up beside me and nuzzles my hand, which is his way of asking me to give him some food. I scratch his ears absently.

The sound of the door—from the garage into the kitchen—opening makes all of us turn. Mara is walking into the house. Her eyes find mine and I go to her, wrapping her in my arms.

"I knew you'd be here," she says.

I fight the lump in my throat, asking, "Are you okay?"

"I'm fine."

I pull back so I can look at her. Her mascara is a little smeared, but other than that, she looks just like always. I kiss her and pull her back into my arms.

"I don't know if it just hasn't hit me yet, but I'm feeling just fine," she says. "Is that lasagna in the oven?"

Suki laughs. "Yes. If you're hungry, you're in the right place."

"I'm starving."

I reluctantly release Mara so she can hug Suki, then Carter.

"He's going to jail, right?" Suki asks.

Mara nods. "Yeah. He'll get prison time."

"Are you sure that job is safe?"

"Nothing's ever completely safe," Mara says. "That's where I want to be, though. I like it so much better than my corporate job. Even when I'm being held hostage."

"Too soon," I say, shaking my head. "That shit took about a decade off my life."

"I feel like eating a giant piece of lasagna and then sleeping for about ten hours," she says. "My boss told me not to come in tomorrow." She gives me a hopeful look. "Can we binge an entire season of a show? Please?"

I shake my head, amazed at how quickly she seems to have moved on from what happened.

"We can do anything you want, babe."

"Can we watch *Love Island*?"

"Absolutely."

CHAPTER TWENTY-TWO

Mara

"MARA, it's real. I went to the bank and the teller confirmed it's a real check."

My mom is crying, and I am too. I'm sitting in a recliner in Leo's living room, Birdie on my lap. We've watched four episodes of *Love Island*, but we're on a break because he had to go to a team meeting even though he's still rehabbing his knee.

"You guys deserve it, Mom."

"This is our future son-in-law, isn't it? The card he sent with the check said, 'Thank you for raising such an incredible daughter.'"

That gets me. I told Bash our two-hundred-fifty-thousand deal was off, and this is the first I'm hearing about him sending my parents a check. It's for three hundred thousand, an amount that will change their lives.

I stop petting Birdie, and she gives me a pleading look until I start back up. She really is the sweetest dog. All she wants is to be near someone at all times, preferably while being petted and talked to.

"Mara, be honest with me. Is he buying your virginity? Your father and I won't support that."

I scoff. "Mom, that ship sailed a long time ago."

"Well, women these days are having surgeries to become virgins again. I saw it online. It's called a hymenoplasty. Can you imagine?"

"Ugh, no. Just no."

The clinking sound of dishes in the background tells me she's unloading the dishwasher. I didn't tell her about Drake Harn; it would only worry my parents and I don't want that.

"Have you seen that movie *Indecent Proposal*? The marriage was ruined. There's no amount of money that's worth selling your body for."

I don't bother explaining to her that the movie was fictional. "There's no body selling going on here, Mom. I promise. Leo just wanted to do something nice for you guys."

"Nice?" She laughs. "This is far more than nice. We're going to be able to pay off our house. I haven't known life without a mortgage payment in more than thirty years."

"I'm so happy for you guys."

"I may even go get my hair done. I've been cutting it myself for years."

"You should, Mom. Treat yourself."

"I was thinking maybe we could go together when you're home for Christmas. You can tell the stylist how to cut it. I don't know what's in style."

I smile, because she's been wearing her hair in a short bob for more than twenty years. I can't imagine her with any other haircut.

"What's in style is hair that makes you feel good. Don't worry about your hair looking like anyone else's. And a day at a salon with you sounds amazing, but I can only come for Christmas Eve and Christmas. Salons aren't open then."

"You're bringing Leo, aren't you?"

I cringe. I adore Leo, but our relationship is still very new. I assume he'll want to spend Christmas with his own family.

"I don't think we're at that stage of the relationship yet, Mom."

"If he loves our daughter enough to send us three hundred thousand dollars as thanks for raising her, surely he at least wants to meet us."

"Yes, but—"

"But nothing. Bring him home to meet your parents."

She doesn't ask for much. It's a lot to ask of him to miss the holiday with his family to be with a woman he hasn't even been dating for a month, though.

"I'll talk to him, but I can't promise anything."

"Well, I need to know soon. I bought a ten-pound turkey, but I'll need a bigger one if he's coming. I assume hockey players have big appetites. I'll need at least a fifteen-pound one. And they're all picked over at the meat market."

Birdie huffs out a sigh from my lap. Can she hear my mom? Is she smarter than I realized?

"Mom, he won't eat five pounds of turkey. I don't even know if he'll be able to come."

"It's in four days. I should make another apple pie, too. Does he like apple pie?"

"I don't know. Don't worry about making extra food for him; whatever you have will be fine."

"Aunt Rhonda is making her sweet potato casserole and it has walnuts. He's not allergic, is he?"

I roll my eyes. "Mom, let me talk to him when he gets home."

"Home?" she practically yells. "Are you two living together? You know how your father and I feel about that."

My day of relaxing and recovering has taken a stressful turn. I turn on the TV, open the YouTube app, and search for a video of a doorbell ringing.

"No, we aren't living together. He's at a team meeting and I'm at his house with his dog. That's all I meant."

"Why aren't you at work?"

"I have a day off." I play a video, turning up the volume. "Mom, there's someone at the door. I have to answer it. I'll let you know later today about Christmas."

"Don't open it. I just watched a show about a rapist who dresses like a delivery driver."

"It's someone I know. I have to go, Mom. Love you."

"Love you too, honey."

———

"CHECK THIS OUT." Leo tosses his keys on the kitchen counter when he gets back a couple of hours later, looking excited.

He bends his knee and lifts it up, then puts his foot back on the ground and gets into a squatting position. "I couldn't do that without pain before."

"That's great!"

"The rest and ice are helping."

"I'm so glad."

He's following all the doctor's instructions for rehab, hoping to avoid surgery and be back on the ice in as little as four weeks. Surgery would mean a much longer absence from playing hockey.

I give him a quick kiss and he wraps me in a hug, his clean, masculine scent and strong arms calming me.

"My parents got the check," I say, pulling away to look into his eyes. "They're so grateful. You didn't have to do that."

His lips pull up in a smile. "I did it because I wanted to."

"It means the world to me. You changed their lives."

"It was a small thank you for raising the woman I love."

My lips part with surprise. It's soon, but I'm feeling it, too. I was just too afraid to say the words in case he's not there yet.

"Really?" Tears well in my eyes.

He kisses me. "Really."

"I love you, too, Leo. I know we just got together, but ... I never get tired of you. That's never happened to me before."

The corners of his eyes crinkle when he smiles. "I'm sure you'll get tired of me at some point. But that doesn't mean we're not great together."

"I'm easily annoyed," I admit.

"I'm aware. I used to annoy you by existing."

He puts his hands on my hips, pulling me close. I put my palms on his chest, a smile tugging at my lips.

"I used to annoy you pretty easily, too."

"Now you're my girl, though. It was worth all the fighting, wasn't it?"

I never thought I wanted to be any man's *girl*. But I love the sound of him calling me that.

"So worth it." I take a deep breath, my smile dropping. "I know this is unlikely to happen, and I totally get that. We just started ... dating? Have we had an official date yet?"

"No, but I plan to fix that very soon."

"Right. Well, when I talked to my mom earlier, she asked me to bring you home with me for Christmas. I can definitely tell her no, but she wanted me to ask you."

He considers. "I'm going to see my parents on Christmas Day."

"I know, I get it. Don't worry about it."

"What if we go see my parents on Christmas Eve and yours on Christmas Day?"

I think about it for a second, then nod. "We could. My mom would be over the moon. But wouldn't your family be like, 'Who is this and why is she here when you've only been with her for like ten minutes?'"

"Nah. If I tell them you're important to me, that's all that matters."

"And your family is in Indianapolis, right?"

"A suburb. About forty-five minutes out of the city. We'll make it work."

I furrow my brow. "My mom can be a lot."

"I'd expect no less from the woman who raised you."

I laugh. "She's a different *lot* than I am. I'm a very toned-down version of myself around my family."

"It'll be good. My parents will be thrilled to meet you."

Meeting his parents. It's a big step, but I feel ready. I want them to like me.

His expression turns serious. "I need to tell you something. It's not easy for me to talk about." He shakes his head and looks away. "I had an older brother. Kyle. He died of leukemia when I was eleven and he was thirteen."

My heart cracks in half. "Leo. God, I'm so sorry your family went through that."

"It was ..." He clears his throat, emotional. "The hardest thing any of us has ever experienced. But Kyle was adamant that he wanted us to keep living and he happy."

I fight the well of emotion in my throat. "He was only thirteen, and he thought like that?"

"Cancer made him grow up fast. It was brutal. But my parents ... They still talk about him. There are pictures of him all over their house. I just want you to know so you aren't surprised."

I nod. "I appreciate that. I'd love to hear about him."

"It's weird. I don't like bringing him up myself, but I like hearing my parents talk about him. When I'm home, I feel him there. I feel the good times and the bad ones. I like seeing pictures of him at their house, even though it would be too painful for me to put a picture up in my own. I leave it all there when I go. It's just how I live with it."

"I get that. There's no right or wrong there. You just do what feels best to you."

He gives me a sheepish look. "I'm going to warn you —my mom is desperate for grandchildren. If I tell her not to say anything, she'll still sneak in hints."

I put my hands on his shoulders, grinning. "Don't worry. I can handle your mom. The only big question we need to worry about right now is what we're going to eat while we finish *Love Island*."

"New relationship rule—if you're held hostage, you

get to choose where to order food from for forty-eight hours after."

I arch a brow, impressed. "Look at you, joking about it just like me. I'm going with Chinese."

"I'll order the food and change back into my sweats."

"I'll get the show ready. Teamwork makes the dream work."

He kisses my forehead. "We better relax while we can. I have a feeling the holidays might be ... interesting this year."

CHAPTER TWENTY-THREE

Leo

"MARA, you're so beautiful. I wonder if your kids will get your pretty brown eyes."

I sigh softly, squeezing Mara's hand. My parents just met Mara five minutes ago, and my mom's already dropping hints about our future children.

"You're so sweet, thank you," Mara says. "Everyone says I look just like my mom."

"Finally settling down, Leo?" my Uncle Rob asks, shaking my hand in greeting. "It's about time. Puck bunnies keep your bed warm, but they don't have dinner waiting when you get home."

"Hey, Uncle Rob."

It's the first time I've brought a woman home, and my family is excited to say the least. Family members who weren't supposed to come until tomorrow decided to come early since Mara and I won't be here then. My parents' modest ranch is loud and festive, with sixteen extended family members here. Mara's meeting my grandparents, aunts, uncles, cousins, and my cousins' kids.

"What do you do for a living, Mara?" my dad asks.

While the kids play, the adults are congregated in the living room and kitchen, talking and snacking on food my mom has out. When I told her Mara and I were coming for Christmas Eve, she quickly planned a full celebration. My dad smoked two briskets and Mom made a bunch of sides and appetizers.

"I'm an assistant state's attorney. I work in the traffic division."

"An attorney?" My dad gives me an approving look. "So she's Smart *and* beautiful."

"She's also funny and compassionate," I say. "I'm still not sure what she sees in me."

"Well, you're rich," my cousin Chelsea says.

That gets some weak laughs. I know Mara must be working overtime to hold back the quips that usually fly out of her mouth after comments like that.

My parents don't serve alcohol in their house, so she's meeting my family without the assistance of wine. I have a bottle of her favorite wine packed in my suitcase for later. We told my parents we're staying at her parents' house tonight and her parents we're staying at my parents' house tonight. But really, we're staying at a hotel. Overnight would be too much for the first time meeting each other's families.

"So what's up with your knee, Leo?" my cousin Tony asks.

"Torn meniscus. I'm rehabbing it."

"Are you getting surgery?"

"As of now, no. But if rehab doesn't work, I might have to."

He furrows his brow. "That's gotta be rough, missing games."

"It is?"

"Do you still get paid for games you don't play in?" Chelsea asks.

"Yeah."

My mom comes in and sits on the arm of the recliner my dad is sitting in. She does that when she's busy in the kitchen, but eager to be included in the living room conversation.

"So, Mara, how did you and Leo meet?" Mom asks.

Mara smiles at me. "We've known each other for a while. My friend Suki married Leo's friend Carter, and we all spend a lot of time together."

"Was it love at first sight?"

I squeeze her hand, rubbing my thumb over her knuckles. "Not exactly."

"I didn't fully appreciate Leo at first," Mara says.

Chelsea laughs hard at that. "Oh, I love it. Did you think he was arrogant? He comes off arrogant."

I flick a glare at my cousin. The two of us aren't even close, but she likes to think she's an expert on me. I've gotten her great seats to every Crush game she's ever asked for tickets to, sometimes paying for them because I couldn't get them from the team, and she's still not all that nice to me.

"I just didn't know him yet," Mara says, giving me an affectionate look. "To know Leo is to love him."

My mom puts her palms on her chest, smiling. "I knew Leo would be smart and wait for the right woman. You two make such a beautiful couple." She presses her lips together before blurting, "Do you want kids, Mara?"

"Mom." I give her a pointed look. "That question's not appropriate right now."

Mara gives my hand a squeeze. "I don't mind. I do want kids. Suki and Carter have three girls and I love them to pieces. So does Leo."

"Oh, a little girl," my mom says wistfully. "I'm a mom of two boys. I can't imagine. The little dresses and pigtails ..."

"Slow down, Marie," my mom's sister Maggie says. "We just met her."

Mom laughs. "I know. Sorry, Mara."

Mara waves a hand. "It's okay. My mom feels the same way."

Mom gets up from the arm of the chair. "I'd love to hear all about your parents. Do you mind coming into the kitchen so we can talk while I finish up some food?"

"Of course." Mara stands. "One of my best friends is a chef at his own restaurant. I don't know a lot about cooking, but I'm a good assistant."

While the rest of the family in the living room talks,

I keep one ear on the conversation in here and another on the kitchen. I can't make out what my mom and Mara are saying to each other, but there's a lot of laughter.

My mom deserves this. She's proud of me, but I have to travel so much that I don't make it home a lot. I'm going to invite my parents to come see me more often so Mara can get to know them, and vice versa.

No games. Mara and I are on the same page about that. I finally found someone I'm crazy about, and I'm not wasting any time on games.

———

THE NEXT MORNING, Mara and I are in bed, her cheeks flushed and her smile satisfied.

"Merry Christmas," she whispers.

"Merry Christmas," I whisper back, kissing her.

"I got you something."

"What?" I lower my brows, brushing a section of hair away from her face. "You're my gift, babe. You're all I need."

Her smile is a mix of shy and amused as she says, "I'm giving it to you now."

She gets out of bed and I admire her curves as she digs through her suitcase. We road-tripped to my parents' house, but I've chartered us a flight to go see her parents. It's costing a mint, but it'll be worth it for the time it'll save us.

"I don't know if you'll like it, but I happen to love it."

"That's all that matters," I quip.

"Close your eyes."

I fold my hands behind my head, propping myself up and closing my eyes.

"Okay, open."

I squint; the lighting in the room dim. She's holding an article of clothing out in front of her.

"Is that a hockey sweater?"

"Here." She walks over to switch on a lamp, then holds it out in front of her again. "Cuyahoga County, which I work for, has a county seal, and that's what this is."

It's embroidered on the front of the jersey, just like my team logo is on mine.

She flips the sweater around. It says "Torres"—her last name—and has the number sixty-nine.

"I got you a jersey with my name on it," she says. "Just like I have one with yours."

I laugh heartily and sit up. "Babe. That's fucking awesome. I love it."

"You do?"

"I do. I'll wear the hell out of that."

"I had to put my favorite number on it."

"I noticed." I slide to the side of the bed and get up, walking over to kiss her. "Thank you, babe. I love it."

I take it from her hands and hold it up in front of my chest. She smiles, looking giddy.

"Dex and Harry said you'd pretend to like it, but Suki said you'd really like it."

I put it on.

"Oh, I love it!" she says. "I'd take a picture, but your dick's hanging out, so let's wait on that."

I show her the back, and she squeals with excitement. "The world will know you're all mine when you wear that."

"They'll know all the time, because I'll tell everyone I see."

I go over to my suitcase and take out a small box and a larger one, passing her the smaller one first. "For you."

Her smile drops away. "Leo, no. What you did for my parents was all the gift I could ever ask for."

"Just open it. This is something I picked out for you myself, and it's okay if you don't like it, it's exchangeable."

My heart hammers nervously as she opens it. I bought it on my recent road trip to New York, and I showed Suki a picture before I finalized the purchase. She said she thought Mara would love it.

"Oh my God." Mara has the blue Tiffany box unwrapped. "You shouldn't have done this."

"Open it." It's all I can do not to grab it and open it myself.

She flips open the box and inhales sharply. "Oh, Leo. Oh wow." Tears shine in her eyes when she looks up at me. "It's so beautiful. You picked this out?"

I nod. It's a rose gold necklace with a circular

pendant, the pendant covered with little diamonds. Mara doesn't wear earrings, and Suki said she doesn't like bracelets, so I went with a necklace.

"I've never even seen anything so gorgeous," she says. "Is this really happening?"

"I'll help you put it on in a second, but first—" I pass her the larger box.

She shakes her head. "Leo, seriously. I know you have a lot of money, but I don't want you to spend so much on me. This is just us, it's not about money."

"I got you these gifts because I wanted to. I'm so damned happy with you, Mara, and that's a big deal for me. You're a big deal. And I could barely stand knowing this was in my suitcase, because I wanted to give it to you early so much. Now open it."

She gives me a quick kiss. "I'm happy, too. You're amazing."

This gift is a sure thing, because Suki chose it. When I asked her what I could get Mara that would knock her socks off, she sent me a link to this.

"No!" Mara cries when she sees the logo on the cardboard box. "No, you didn't!"

She flips off the lid and pushes the tissue aside.

"My dream black Louboutin booties," she says softly. "This is ... I'm ..." She takes out one of the booties and sniffs it. "This is what heaven smells like."

"Suki said you've been wanting those."

She shakes her head. "I never actually thought I'd own a pair of Louboutins. I can't even afford the used ones."

Setting the box on the bed, she hugs me. "I'm overwhelmed. Thank you so much."

"We're just getting started, babe. There are many more good times ahead for us."

———

"WE COULDN'T HAVE ASKED for anything more in a daughter," Mara's dad says to me later that morning. "She's the best thing I've ever done."

Nick Torres isn't what I expected. He's paralyzed from the waist down, but I forgot about that within the first ten minutes of talking to him. He's wearing a Wounded Warrior Project baseball hat, a flannel and jeans. His eyes are warm and he's easy to talk to.

"You and your wife have done an incredible job," I say.

After we finished eating and exchanging gifts, Nick asked to talk to me privately. He wheeled his chair into a sunroom off the kitchen, closing the double glass doors so we could talk alone.

"Why do you love my daughter?" he asks me.

"She challenges me and supports me. I don't know how she manages to do both those things at once, but she does. She makes me laugh, and she stands up for people who can't stand up for themselves. She's strong, but she lets herself be vulnerable enough to need me. Just like I need her."

He nods, an emotion I can't place in his eyes.

"Life doesn't always go like you think it's going to."

He gestures at his legs. "I never saw this coming. But my wife—she never doubted me. She thinks I'm strong, so I am."

I feel like he has more to say, so I wait quietly.

"If someone had told me twenty years ago that I'd be stuck in a wheelchair for the rest of my life at age thirty-seven, and that I'd be happy with my life, I wouldn't have believed it. I would've thought my life was over. But my wife and daughter—they're my reasons."

"I know I don't have your years of wisdom and experience, but Mara is becoming my reason. I love her. I'm devoted to her."

He smiles softly. "She deserves that. And as long as you're good to her, you're family to us."

"Thank you, sir. That means a lot."

"Thank you for the money. I thought I'd be too proud to accept it, but when I saw the weight it took from my wife's shoulders, I knew I had to swallow my pride."

"I don't expect that to buy me goodwill. It was a gift, with no expectations."

Mara is standing in front of the glass doors, cringing. I smile at her and Nick turns, smiling and waving for her to come in.

"Did you scare him off, Dad?" she cracks.

"I let him know I can kick his ass if he hurts my daughter, legs or no legs."

I put my palms up. "Won't be necessary, I promise."

Mara's mom walks into the room carrying a pie. "I

thought we'd have dessert in here. But first, can I ask Aunt Rhonda to take a picture of all of us for Facebook?"

Mara and I exchange a look. We haven't gone social media official, but I can't think of a better way to do it than this, with her parents, while I'm wearing the jersey she gave me for Christmas and she's wearing the necklace and booties I got her.

"You bet," I say, standing up.

Mara takes my hand and leads me from the room, going to stand in front of the Christmas tree in the living room. While we wait for her parents to come into the room, she stands beside me, grinning.

"Can you believe this?" she says.

I don't have to ask to know what she means. Us. This. The drastic difference between our feelings for each other this Christmas and last Christmas.

"I think it was inevitable, we just took our time getting here," I say, kissing her.

EPILOGUE

Six Months Later

MARA

BASH AND LAINEY are getting married in paradise. The archway behind the officiant is covered with purple and white flowers, the ocean a sparkling backdrop.

They wanted to get married at sunset, so the setting of the sun could represent the end of their separate lives and the start of their new one together as a married couple.

A year ago, I would have secretly cackled about that being cheesy. But since I fell hopelessly in love with Leo, I get it. We're borderline ridiculous sometimes. We rub noses when we're alone and no one can make fun of us. He leaves love notes taped to my steering wheel when he has to leave before sunrise for road trips. I sleep in his t-shirts because they smell like him.

"If I can't have a *Pretty in Pink* theme, at least I still get to be pretty," Dex says, admiring his reflection in the mirror.

I roll my eyes at him, smiling. The rest of the bridal party overruled him on *Pretty in Pink*, because purple is Lainey's color and it's her wedding. The maid of honor, Lily, is wearing a pale-lavender dress with a halter neck. Suki and I are both wearing the same style of dress in the sleeveless version. Harry and Dex are wearing white tuxes with purple bow ties that match the dresses.

"Who's out there now?" Lainey asks, a line of worry between her brows.

I smooth out the line with my fingertip while Dex peeks around the corner from where the bridal party is waiting out of sight from the handful of guests.

"No fretting on your wedding day," I say.

"I don't want to be sweating in the photos," she says. "Let's fucking go."

She's just nervous, like any bride would be. But Suki has planned this day down to the smallest detail, and Lainey is a radiant bride. Her bright-red hair is smooth and straight, a crown of tropical flowers sitting on top. Her dress is flowy and white, with a cinched waist and a plunging neckline. The vibe is island princess, and it's perfection.

"The groomsmen are out there," Dex says. "My lord, Mara, I'm jealous of the railings you get from that absolute unit of a man. He's wearing the fuck out of that tux."

"Focus, Dex!" Lainey barks.

"Okay ... there's Bash, he's there with the grooms-men. He's drinking from a flask."

"What?"

"Kidding. That would be funny, though. The officiant is up there. Should I signal your dad?"

She takes a deep breath in and blows it out. "Yes. I'm ready."

She turns to her friend Lily. "Does my face look sweaty?"

"It's perfect. You are a stunning bride."

"Thank you."

Lainey's dad comes and says a few words to her that make them both teary, and then the music starts up. That's our cue to walk down the aisle and take our places.

Olivia, Charlotte, and Hallie are all flower girls. Hallie goes first, the guests smiling when they see her in her frilly lavender dress. She was adamant that her dress be "fancy." She drops her white petals onto the sandy beach as she walks, running out before she's halfway down the aisle.

"Look at her, trying to look like she planned it that way," Suki cracks.

Charlotte goes next, followed by Olivia. Then it's Harry's turn.

Harry's boyfriend Aden is one of the guests. They're still going strong. Now that the hockey season is over, we're all staying in Hawaii for a vacation after the wedding. Bash and Lainey will be with us for a couple of days here on Maui, and then they're moving on to Kauai, where they have a luxury treehouse rented for a week.

Dex follows Harry, and I try to angle my neck in front of the fan while I watch him walk. My hair is all up, but my neck is still sweaty. I don't know why I'm a little nervous—I'm just a bridesmaid. I don't have to worry about tripping because we're all wearing flip-flops in the sand.

When it's my turn to walk, I hold my bouquet of lilies in front of me, my eyes locking onto Leo. My stomach flutters nervously when he smiles at me.

So *that's* why I'm nervous. It's because I'm walking down an aisle toward Leo. Granted, it's not *the* aisle—we're incredibly happy but not ready for engagement yet. But it's an aisle, and I'm getting a preview of what I hope for us one day.

Our first six months together have been a dream. He missed five weeks of his season rehabbing his knee and didn't have to get surgery. We spent as much of his time away from his team as we could together. I gave up my apartment and officially moved in with him, so his house no longer looks like a model unit that no one lives in.

Things just fell into place during that time. We became a couple in every way. It was hard when he had to go back to work, but also okay, because he was so excited to be returning to his team to play the game he loves.

I can hear the crashing of waves over the music, and it calms me. I'm kind of a wave myself. I have highs and lows. I can be loud and dramatic. But I'm also steady.

Leo has helped my inner confidence grow. I always looked confident on the outside, but now I feel more sure of who I am and what I want than I ever have.

I'm walking toward what I want. My future. And his eyes promise me everything I never even dreamed I'd have.

WANT MORE?

The next book in the Love on the Line series is A Deal with the Defender.

ABOUT THE AUTHOR

Brenda Rothert lives in Central Illinois with her husband, children and three dogs. She loves to hear from readers through her website or her Facebook group, Rothert's Readers.

Keep up with all the latest on Brenda's books and get bonus content by signing up for her newsletter at brendarothert.com/subscribe.

www.ingramcontent.com/pod-product-compliance
Lightning Source LLC
Chambersburg PA
CBHW011515100726
47899CB00010BD/3371